BLUE JEAN

BLUE JEAN

M. J. SMITH

Morning Joy Media
Spring City, Pennsylvania

Thank you Angie Batluck for your friendship, for reading every draft, and for your insightful quote choices. Thank you Karen Heard for your friendship and for another beautiful cover design. Thank you Debbie Capeci for your editing and publishing expertise and for seeing the potential in my writing. And thank you God for Your loving-kindness and for never letting me go.

Published by Morning Joy Media.

Visit www.morningjoymedia.com for more information on bulk discounts and special promotions, or e-mail your questions to info@morningjoymedia.com.

Cover design: Karen Heard | Chalk Design
Interior design: Debbie Capeci

Smith, Marijo.
  Blue Jean / by Marijo Smith.

Summary:

After a cross-country move, Scott, Maggie, and their infant daughter, Abby, find themselves far from family and friends. Maggie struggles with anger against her husband for removing her from all she knows. She meets an elderly neighbor, Jean, who helps Maggie see into her own heart as Jean reveals the secrets of each of the neighborhood's former residents.

 ISBN 978-1-937107-39-0 (paperback)
 ISBN 978-1-937107-40-6 (ebook)

 1. Neighborhoods—Fiction. 2. Pennsylvania—Reading. 3. Families. 4. Older women—Fiction. I. Title.

Printed in the United States of America

To my husband, Jim, and to my daughter, Ali.
Thank you for all of the love and joy you have brought into my life.

CHAPTER 1

Home should be an oratorio of the memory, singing to all our
after life melodies and harmonies of old-remembered joy.

—Henry Ward Beecher

Scott stood in his bedroom staring at the clothing in his closet, deciding between two jackets for his dinner with the college president. He had worked hard on his doctorate in pharmacogenomics and after coming in second for the professorship at the University of Montana to a candidate who had written three books on the personalization of medicine, the job in Pennsylvania turned out to be a blessing, or at least he thought so at first. Taking Maggie away from her family and friends in Montana proved to be hard on their marriage. Scott was doing everything he could to make his marriage work. It was becoming all one-sided, however. Maggie didn't seem to care that their relationship was falling apart.

The doorbell rang, interrupting his thoughts. As Scott walked down the stairs to the front door, Maggie stood holding the front door open. Scott noticed a distinguished-looking woman on the front porch talking to his wife.

Maggie said to the woman, "Really, you can come in. I'd love for you to see the house."

The woman smiled and shook her head no, "We just wanted to stop by—we don't live around here anymore, but we were at a funeral in town and my son suggested we see the house one more time."

Shaking the woman's hand, Maggie replied, "It was really nice to meet you." She closed the door and Scott asked, "Who was that?"

"That was Joy. She and her family lived in our house about twenty years ago. They wanted to introduce themselves to us. I said they could see the house, but Joy said no."

Scott looked out one of the sets of French doors in the living room. "They're still on the sidewalk. Why don't we give it one more try and invite them in."

Maggie and Scott appeared on the front porch waving Joy and her family up to the house. Joy began jumping up and down, and arm-in-arm the group climbed the many stairs to the white cottage house with black shutters and red front door.

Joy said, "You have made us so happy. Thank you so much for welcoming us."

The introductions went around as excited voices from Joy's family intermingled with one another, "Remember the family dinners in the dining room...I love the color you used in here...I remember when Jimmy and his friends used to slide down the stairs...Sis, what parties we used to have in the living room...I forgot what a gorgeous view there is from up here."

Maggie and Scott listened to the stories, the memories of the good times for Joy and her family. A happy family. As the tour of the house came to an end, the guests walked out of the house in single file with Joy last. Before she stepped onto the front porch, Joy looked back over her shoulder, and with a tone of satisfaction she said, "This is still a happy home."

Maggie's smile hid her pain as she thought, *If you only knew.*

CHAPTER 2

Are the days of winter sunshine just as sad for you, too?
When it is misty, in the evenings, and I am out walking by myself,
it seems to me that the rain is falling through my heart
and causing it to crumble into ruins.

– Gustave Flaubert

Maggie believed she would be able to handle the move. She thought she had what it takes to be a good wife, but the more she thought about their new baby girl growing up not knowing any grandparents or aunts and uncles, the more obvious the bitterness she felt toward her husband became. She thought she could suppress it, hide it, fool Scott into believing she wasn't beginning to hate him, but the very sight of her husband filled her with anger. One way for Scott to make Maggie's resentment even worse was doing anything nice or special for her. Then her anger spilled over, and even if her words were kind, the tone she used was not. There were times Maggie felt better, felt like she didn't hate her husband, but that was only when he was at work, away from their home. Alone with their daughter, she was happy and content.

If Scott had gotten the job at the University of Montana, Maggie understood they would need to move from Bigfork to Missoula. A two-hour commute each way each day would be too much, and she was sure they could find a nice home in Missoula. She shouldn't have started making plans so soon, shouldn't have gotten her hopes up. She would miss Bigfork; it was an artists' town, small and cozy with shops, restaurants, Flathead Lake, the Swan River; there was always something to do. Missoula had its own personality, too, and the best part: she would still be in Montana surrounded by her friends and family.

But after a month in Wyomissing Hills, Pennsylvania, Maggie realized they were here to stay. She had spent the month painting the inside of the house and decorating. Once in a while, Maggie would explore the neighborhood, especially when she couldn't get Abby to sleep. She would take Abby for a drive and that always worked. Soon her daughter would be sleeping peacefully and Maggie would carefully carry her back into the house to her crib. On these drives she noticed this was a long-established neighborhood with character-filled old homes. Now that the weather was getting a bit warmer, it was time to get out of the house, take Abby for a walk in her stroller and explore the area on foot. She had not yet met anyone, choosing to keep to herself.

Maggie put warm clothes and a jacket on Abby, finding it hard to believe she was three months old already. She had grown so much in such little time. Their families were grateful for the FaceTime chats and many pictures they sent of Abby. It helped them feel like they were a part of Abby's life. Maggie got her camera out to record this moment, "Look here, Abby. Smile for Mommy. Grammy and Pop-Pop will love to see you all bundled up for our walk." Smiling she said, "The picture is perfect, beautiful girl."

The pair took a left out of the driveway heading down a street lined with oak trees. The branches were bare, allowing for an abundance of sunshine. The air was still brisk, but it felt good to be out of the house. Maggie found her way to the bottom of the hill and turned right. All the houses were so different from one another, some stone, some brick, but each one offering its own charm. *This area must have looked like a Christmas card when everyone decorated for the holidays.* Maggie missed the lights, wreaths, and greens which must have adorned the old homes during the holidays, but she was glad to spend one last Christmas with her family in Montana and having a newborn made the celebration even happier.

After rounding the next corner, Maggie started up the hill exerting a bit more effort pushing the stroller. As she came up behind the house that was across the street from her home, she saw an elderly woman sweeping the side porch. The woman waved and yelled across the yard, "Hi there, honey. I think you're my new neighbor. Come on over." Maggie wheeled Abby's stroller down the walkway. The woman stuck out her hand, "I'm Jean."

"Hi, I'm Maggie and this is Abby," she said, motioning to her sleeping daughter.

"Well, well. It's nice to finally meet the both of you. I thought you would never come out of your house. I was getting fit to walk those steps, but I didn't know how I'd do it. My legs don't hold me the way they used to, and I haven't been up to your house since my friends lived there some forty years ago."

"Oh, do you mean Joy and her family?"

Laughing, Jean said, "No dear. Joy is much younger than I am, but thank you anyway for the compliment. Joy moved in some time after my friends moved away. Honey, do I have some stories about your house."

Maggie's ears perked up. "Really?"

"Yes. Your house was the party house."

"My house?"

"I'm talking grand piano in the front room. Singing and dancing spilling out onto the front porch. Listen, why don't I make us some coffee, seeing that your daughter is still asleep, and I'll tell you about it."

Maggie sat in Jean's dining room, taking in the antique furnishings. "I really like this furniture. Is it antique?"

"It was my parents' furniture, so I'd say it's pretty old, but nothing anyone else would want. My living room looks the same as it did on the first day Marty and I moved here."

"Is Marty your husband?"

"Yes, dear. He passed away twenty years ago. Marty was a good man and I still miss him. We had so much fun together. I had the best life a girl could have and now here I am an old woman."

Trying her best to make Jean feel better, Maggie offered, "You look great, Jean. Your nails are painted, your hair's done, and I love that shade of lipstick you're wearing."

"Oh, please. I do all this in case I fall over in my house and those emergency guys have to come in and take me away. I don't want anyone to see me without my make-up. Marty never saw me without make-up, and I'm not going to have some good-looking young guy come running into my house with an oxygen tank and a stretcher and here I am without my hair fixed and my face looking beautiful."

Jean began laughing and then added, "Oh, Maggie. It's no fun getting old. My eyes are going on me. I get up to go to the bathroom every half hour at night. I can't walk without a cane. A cane. Imagine. At least when Marty died I still had some of my sexy-actress looks left. Even though I wasn't an actress, mind you, I still looked like one. If he could come back for a visit, he wouldn't recognize me. Heck, I don't recognize me. All right, enough about me. Let's hear about you. Where did you move from?"

"We moved from Montana."

"Well, I'll be, here I have a real-life cowgirl in my house."

That made Maggie smile. "I guess I was kind of a cowgirl. Both my husband and I were outdoorsy. When we were in college, my summer job was to lead horseback trail rides through parts of Glacier National Park, and Scott taught people how to fly fish."

Jean's eyes lit up. "Imagine, real-life adventurers right across the street from me, and one of them a horse lover. I used to show horses."

Maggie was beginning to feel a connection to this woman. Jean's words would make anyone think she was getting ready to die, but the energy and excitement in her voice said her neighbor and new friend had a lot of life left in her.

Jean said, "I met Marty at one of my horse shows."

Maggie nearly jumped up, "I met Scott on one of my trail tours."

"We have a lot in common, my young friend."

As Jean uttered the last syllable, Abby began to cry. "Honey, it looks like you need to get your baby daughter back home for her bottle. She sounds like a hungry little one."

"Yes, I'm sure she is starving. This was the longest Abby's slept in a while."

"Well, then you'll have to come back soon so we can continue our talk. I have a lot to share with you, and I think you probably have a lot to share with me."

Maggie smiled. "I would love to hear all your stories. I can't wait to visit with you again."

"You are welcome any time, dear."

When Maggie pushed the stroller out of Jean's house, the air was damp and she wished she were back inside with Jean's warmth wrapped around her. Scott's return drew near. Maggie never envisioned a time would come when she wouldn't want to see her husband at the end of the day, never thought she would feel dread in place of the excitement that used to be in her heart.

CHAPTER 3

For after all, the best thing one can do
when it is raining is let it rain.
— Henry Wadsworth Longfellow

Driving home after another successful day of work with his research taking hold and the college administration beginning to take notice, Scott still knew he would face the opposite at home. It had been a gradual decline. During the first week in Pennsylvania, Scott noticed as he talked with Maggie that her voice had lost some of its joy. No matter what the conversation, her tone became nondescript. But at least at that point Maggie was still talking to him. As the weeks went on, she stopped cooking, and within a couple of months, she would sit in front of the television and barely look up when he walked into the house. Scott would make himself a sandwich for dinner, and maybe if he wanted something hot, he would heat up a can of soup. Scott wasn't sure what Maggie ate during the day, but he never saw her eat dinner anymore. What a juxtaposition this was. Everything was going well for him at work but felt like a disaster at home.

This wasn't how their life was in Montana. They did everything together. Maggie would open the door for him as he made his way up the walkway, a warm smile on her face, and Abby pressed to her chest. He never got tired of that sight. His wife and daughter. Scott knew how blessed he was to have Maggie. She's beautiful and smart and creative. No matter how Maggie acted toward him, Scott still loved his wife. He wished so much that she would be happy in Pennsylvania. He always thought they could make it through anything as long as they were together, but this move was starting to show that just might not be true.

One morning after an evening of being ignored, Scott didn't think he would be able to take the silent treatment anymore and thought maybe it would be better to have Maggie back with her parents. He thought about telling her if she wanted to go back to Montana, she could. Maybe they could work out their problems long distance, but then Scott looked down at the shelf just above the bathroom sink and saw Abby's pink plastic barrettes next to Maggie's silver one. Maggie and Abby were everything to Scott. He couldn't imagine spending any part of his life without them. That morning Scott made a vow to be patient for as long as was needed.

Scott put a smile on his face as he entered his home. He announced his arrival with, "Hi girls, I'm home." Silence as usual. Gently dropping his briefcase in the dining room, he loosened his tie as he walked down the hallway to the family room. Maggie was sitting on the floor next to Abby, who was on a blanket with her eyes following the gentle motions of her zoo animal mobile. Scott sat down next to Maggie and kissed her on the cheek. He picked his daughter up and held her in his arms. Talking to Abby, Scott said, "Why don't I take my girls out for a nice dinner tonight. We can explore the area."

Maggie wanted to say yes. She desperately wanted her marriage back the way it used to be, but anger and resentment had walled Scott out and trapped her in. Maggie hated the way she treated him. She felt awful for ignoring her husband and the anger she felt toward him made her feel ugly inside and out. Unable once again to dig deep within herself and get back to the fun-loving, vibrant, caring woman Scott had fallen in love with, she instead kept her face toward the floor and shook her head no. Unsurprised, yet undaunted by Maggie's reaction, Scott said, "Okay, we'll go out some other time. If Abby hasn't had her bottle yet, I'll get it for her."

Scott carried Abby into the kitchen where he whispered in his daughter's ear, "Don't worry, sweet pea, Daddy won't give up. We'll have your mommy back soon."

CHAPTER 4

You can't stay in your corner of the Forest waiting for others
to come to you. You have to go to them sometimes.

– Winnie-the-Pooh

The next morning Maggie watched out the window as Scott left to teach his ten o'clock class. She could hardly wait to get Abby ready for her walk, all the while hoping Jean would be up. The morning proved to be a bit of a struggle with Abby fussing over her bottle, then soaking through her diaper and needing a clothing change. Maggie thought she would never get out of the house that day. But the later it got, the better chance she figured she would have to see Jean. After wrapping a blanket around Abby in her fresh outfit and placing her in her stroller, Maggie stepped out the front door and made her way across the street. She hadn't anticipated spending time with anyone but Abby since the move, but now that she knew Jean, she started feeling happy again and looked forward to seeing her new friend.

Just as Maggie hoped, Jean was in her kitchen and when she saw her neighbor, she opened the window. "I just made a pot of coffee. I could drink it all myself, but I really shouldn't. Why don't you and Abby come in for a visit?"

Quickening her step, Maggie made her way to the front door. "I'd love to."

Jean set a place in the dining room for the two of them with antique teacups and saucers. One was white with a tiny blue floral pattern on it, and the other one had a red and black floral pattern with a gold rim. There was a pie cabinet against the far wall with its doors opened to show off Jean's collection of antique teacups. All of them were mismatched, but that is what made them so beautiful. There was something about the oldness of them that tied them together.

"Your teacups are amazing. Where did you get all of these?"

"I've been collecting them through the years. Our first addition was on our honeymoon in France. After that whenever Marty and I would go on vacation, we would stop at antique shops to add to our collection. A few are gifts from my friends and family. It was always fun to have a party or holiday celebration and let everyone choose where they wanted to sit based on which teacup they liked the best. So in keeping with that tradition, where will you be sitting?"

"I really like the blue one."

"Then have a seat, my dear."

"Why don't I help you?"

"Maggie, there isn't much I can do in life anymore. Getting coffee for a friend is one of the few things I can still do. You and Abby make yourselves comfortable. I'll be right back."

Jean walked slowly back into the room carrying a pot of coffee. She rested it on a silver trivet on the dining room table.

Watching her friend maneuver slowly into her chair, Maggie picked up the coffee pot, "If you would allow me to do the honors."

"That would be lovely, dear."

"Do you want cream or sugar?"

"No thank you. I take my coffee black. I've been drinking black coffee ever since I was thirteen. The cream and sugar is for guests."

Maggie poured coffee for herself adding cream to her cup. "I like how you use teacups for coffee. It feels very glamorous."

Laughing amusedly, Jean said, "That's just what I am. Glamorous. Well, I used to be, but not anymore. Just ask my doctor." Jean laughed again thinking about sitting on the white paper on top of the table at the doctor's office.

"You know Maggie, there is something that seems to border on the verge of disrespect making an old woman undress in a cold, sterile examining room, only to put on a terrible excuse for a gown. A gown. For crying out loud, can you imagine calling a stiff, tissue-thin piece of cotton that smells like Clorox a gown? I've worn some true gowns in my day and none of them ever looked like that."

Maggie was laughing, too. "You have a way of explaining things."

"Yes, I do. It's called old age. Now, enough about getting old. As I remember, last time we sat down to talk I found out you were a cowgirl. Now that's glamorous."

"Wearing a tight pair of jeans, leather boots, and a cowboy hat did make my summer job seem glamorous. I felt so free on the trail and even though I was taking groups of people on a tour, there was still a solitude about the job."

"You also told me that's where you met your husband. I haven't seen him up close and I know my eyes are bad, but I can tell he is a very good-looking man. That's one thing I've enjoyed about getting older. I have a keen sense of handsome, and handsome with a good heart, now that is a man you keep hold of. As I remember, you said his name is Scott."

"You have a good memory, Jean. Forget all this about getting old. You have a better memory than I do."

"When it comes to a good-looking man, I have the memory of a twenty-year-old."

"I guess Scott is attractive."

"You guess? Honey, put on some glasses and take a closer look. You are married to a GQ model."

"Okay, okay. I mean, that is what I first noticed about him." Maggie was getting uncomfortable talking about her husband. She didn't want to give away that she and Scott were having problems. "Enough about me, though. I'm really looking forward to hearing about how you met your husband. The horse show sounds like such a romantic place."

"According to Marty, he fell in love with me at first sight at the horse show. He and his friends decided to attend the fair that had become part of the Reading Horse Show, and when Marty saw me on my horse jumping over a fence, he knew I was the one and he made his friends wait around until after the last event in hopes he would get the chance to talk to me. I had a sense for good-looking men back then too, and they sure were cute. Marty stood out among them, and I felt like a million bucks having the best-looking guy at the fair talking to me. He asked me out that day, and we went dancing the next evening. He picked me up in his car. My parents weren't going to let me go, but he was such a gentleman he charmed even my father. After the date we sat on my front porch and talked for hours. We both loved car racing and baseball. We clicked that night, and I never needed to look beyond Marty. He was more than I ever thought I wanted in a man. He was funny and kind. He was a lot of fun. He was a great husband and a great father. It's been years since Marty passed away and sometimes I still miss him as much as the days following his death. I still have my rec room set up for the parties we used to have. Do you want to take a look?"

"I'd love to." Maggie began thinking about her life with Scott. She always wanted them to grow old together. She imagined a marriage much like what Jean had, but it wasn't like that anymore. Sometimes, she could barely imagine spending another week with Scott, and if she was really honest, Maggie could barely stand spending another moment with herself acting the way she was. Maybe to the outside world she seemed fine, but she didn't recognize herself anymore. Who was she becoming? Maggie secretly mourned for the way her life was turning out.

Jean led the way downstairs. There were only a few steps, but Jean still had a lot of difficulty getting to the bottom. Maggie looked around at the wood-paneled bar, the ribbons, and the racing signs and décor. There were flags from NASCAR and Formula One racing. "It looks like you loved all kinds of racing."

"Oh, yes. Marty was a mechanic at a car dealership, and we actually became friends with the owner's son. Being a mechanic at the dealership was a full-time job for Marty, but on the weekends he worked as a mechanic for stock car racing. I've been to many races and gotten to watch racing evolve over the years."

Still holding Abby, Maggie cradled her in her right arm while she picked up the model of a car sitting on the bar. Jean explained, "That is a model of a Grand Prix racing car from the early 1900s. We went to the Moroccan Grand Prix for our tenth anniversary."

"You were in Morocco."

"Yes, Maggie. I traveled the world when I was young. I told you, I had the best life a girl could have."

"It sure sounds like it. I don't even know where to begin looking in here. You have so much memorabilia. I can just imagine how much fun you and all your friends must have had in this room."

"We did have a lot of fun. As we got older, it was the gathering place for holidays with the kids and their families. Most of my photographs from Christmas celebrations were taken down here. I used to hang lights around the windows, and I would put a tree in front of the patio doors. We had a tree upstairs too, in front of the living room window."

Besides the racing mementos, Jean had pictures placed on end tables and shelves of her family and friends. Maggie looked closely at each picture. "You have two sons?"

"Yes. I have two great sons. They are the best, always checking in on me. Bobby is the oldest and Johnny the youngest. They live in Florida with their families."

"I bet you miss them. What took them to Florida?"

"Bobby works for NASA and Johnny is in the military, well, was in the military. He's retired now, but Bobby got him a job at NASA. They spend a lot of time together and their kids are close, so that makes me happy. I get updates all the time. That and they keep trying to get me to move to Florida with them."

"Why don't you go?"

"Oh, Maggie." Jean sighed. "This is my home. I'm too old to pick up and move. Look at all this stuff. Where would I put it? This is where my memories are and I can't imagine being any place else but Wyomissing Hills."

The women began their trek upstairs to the dining room. Jean poured Maggie another cup of coffee. "The Reading Horse Show grounds is a park now, and there's a plaque that commemorates the special event. It would be a nice place to take Abby for a walk. I think both of you would like it. It's only a couple of minutes from here."

"I would love to see it sometime. The ribbons downstairs, they are yours from the horse show?"

Jean's eyes lit up, "All of them. I beat out some hard competition to win those ribbons. They mean a lot to me."

"Abby and I would be honored to have a Reading Horse Show champion take us around the old grounds."

"I would be honored to be the one to do that. We can do it on a day I'm feeling up to walking around outside."

Maggie finished her second cup of coffee. When she glanced outside, she saw Scott's car parked along the curb. She was already looking forward to her next meeting with Jean. "Thank you for everything. I should get back home, but I would love to see you tomorrow. I could bake some blueberry muffins for breakfast."

"That sounds wonderful, but only if you have time, dear. I'll see you in the morning. Give that handsome husband of yours a great big kiss when you see him."

While Maggie was still smiling in seeming affirmation at Jean's last comment, she thought, *If only I could break down these walls and let my husband in again.*

As Maggie pushed the front door open, Scott walked across the foyer to help her.

"I'll get the stroller, Maggie. Just leave it on the porch." Scott folded the stroller and took it downstairs. He noticed that Maggie looked happier today than she had in a while. Perhaps it was a good time to bring up the dinner at the president's house. Scott decided to ease into the topic.

"Did you and Abby have a nice walk?"

Maggie had to start somewhere to get her life back with her husband. This would be it. They could begin to start their life over again. She smiled. "Yes. It was a short walk, though. We spent most of our time at Jean's."

"How was your visit?"

Scott noticed the joy in Maggie's voice as she talked about her day. "It was fun. I enjoy hearing Jean's stories. She has a lot of stories about our house. We really haven't gotten into any of the details yet, but I'm looking forward to hearing them."

"I'm glad you had a good day. I have some good news." This was the most conversation Scott had gotten out of his wife in a long time and his hopes were up that Maggie would agree to the dinner. "The president of the college is having a dinner for the new faculty. It's at his house and spouses are included. I would love for us to go together."

Maggie's happy mood and momentary attempt at getting their marriage back was quickly dashed. "Scott, you know I can't go to the dinner. Who would watch Abby?"

"Some of the professors have daughters who babysit. They would be happy to do this for us."

"I'm not leaving Abby with someone I don't know and since I don't know anyone here, I'm not going."

"Well, what about Jean?"

"Jean isn't at the point in her life where she can really care for a baby for an extended time on her own. She would be the first to say that, although I'm sure she would really want to help us out."

"Maggie, this is an important dinner, and it is equally important for us to get out and do things as a couple."

"Well, you could fly either one of our parents in. Then I would go."

"I would love to be able to do that, I really would, but we can't fly our relatives to Pennsylvania every time we have an event to attend."

"Then, I'm sorry Scott, but it looks like I'm not going. You'll need to do this one solo."

"Maggie, at some point in time we are going to need to go places together."

"I know that, Scott. I really thought we could start working things out between us. Why did you have to ruin it?"

"How did I ruin it, Maggie? How is asking my wife to dinner ruining things?"

She walked into the living room without answering. As soon as she started to soften toward her husband, he had to go and remind her of the home they left. All of their family and friends on the other side of the country.

Scott didn't know what else to say without causing an even bigger argument. He walked up the stairs to their bedroom and changed out of his suit. How long was he supposed to keep up this charade around his colleagues that everything was okay? He would have to make up some story at the dinner as to why Maggie wasn't there and hope no one saw through his excuses.

CHAPTER 5

The bluebird carries the sky on his back.

–Henry David Thoreau

Maggie set her alarm for early the next morning so she would have plenty of time to bake the muffins. She had fresh blueberries in the refrigerator and a stocked pantry with all the ingredients she needed even for the crumb topping. She tiptoed around the kitchen and quietly removed bowls, mixing spoons, and a pan from the cupboard and drawers. Being able to do something for Jean made her happy. She wondered how long it had been since Jean had enjoyed homemade baking. Maggie set the timer on the oven and drew herself a bath, leaving enough time to pack Abby's things for their morning outing Half an hour later while the muffins cooled on a wire rack, she sat on the window seat in the dining room feeding Abby her bottle. Scott walked down the stairs and turned the corner into the dining room. Maggie was just as beautiful as the day they got married, and Scott let the disappointment of the previous evening fall away. "You look beautiful, Magpie."

"Thank you. Abby and I are going to Jean's this morning." Maybe it was the excitement of the day or maybe it was Scott's use of her nickname or the endearing compliment, but her heart warmed for a moment. "There are homemade blueberry muffins on the counter."

"They smell delicious. I'll take one to work and have it with my coffee." He almost added that the smell reminded him of when they lived in Montana and Maggie would go for long walks collecting huckleberries, and he would come home to the smell of muffins and cobbler baking. Scott let that thought go. He didn't want to bring up Montana and ruin the moment, but before he left for the college, he added, "Thank you. This is a nice treat."

Around nine o'clock Maggie put Abby in her stroller and made sure she had the play mat and activity center. Abby loved looking at all the brightly colored toys included in the activity center, and Maggie was really hoping to spend a bit more time with Jean this morning.

She put the muffins on a cupcake stand and sealed it with plastic wrap and then stepped out onto the driveway from the lower level. The steps that wound up the walkway to the front porch were too much to maneuver with the muffins. Usually Maggie would just push the stroller up or down the hill in the grass, but she didn't want to chance dropping the cupcake stand, which was balancing precariously in her left hand. As Maggie got closer to Jean's house, she saw her on the porch and called over to her friend, "Good morning!"

"Perfect timing my dear. Oh, look at Abby, awake and ready for her day."

Jean leaned over the railing on the side of the porch as she reached for a magnolia branch.

"Do you need some help?"

"That would be wonderful. This part gets a little tricky for me."

"What are you doing?"

"Feeding the birds. I'm finished filling the feeder with seed, but I need to put these dried mealworms in that little glass feeder in the yard that's under the bluebird box."

"I love bluebirds. Montana has a light-colored mountain bluebird and I always tried to get them in my yard with no luck. Do you actually have bluebirds living in your yard?"

"Yes I do. It is one of the few joys I have left in my life and I'm thankful for that blessing. Here, take the mealworms and a little bit of this olive oil and put it in the blue glass bowl that's in the stand."

"I understand the mealworms, just not the oil."

"Bluebirds love berries and they love insects. The oil makes the mealworms look alive."

Maggie nodded her head, "Brilliant."

"Thank you for the vote of confidence dear, but any good bird book will give you that bit of information."

Maggie walked through the brown grass that was just beginning to show a bit of life to the side yard where the bluebird box was sitting on top of a wooden post. The feeding bowl was just to the right side of the box, keeping the food source close to the nest. Jean was right, adding the olive oil did make the dried mealworms look alive. Very clever. On her way back to the porch, she noticed a silver gazing globe sitting in the middle of what would soon be a flower garden at the end of the side porch. "Jean, this gazing globe is beautiful."

"Oh, yes. Now let me get the description of it correct. That is my antique glass gazing globe."

"It's beautiful. I didn't notice it before."

"That's because I just took it out of storage this morning. I was feeling surprisingly strong, and with the help of my cane, I was able to lower the bag it was in to the ground from the porch. Then, I hobbled around the side of the yard and placed it in the middle of the garden. And if all that sounds like a production, it was. Everything is a production when you get older."

"I would have helped you with it, Jean."

"I know you would, dear. I still like to do some things for myself no matter how long they take."

"And about how long did that take you?"

"Oh, I would say about half an hour. Seeing your reaction to the globe, I would say it was half an hour well spent. Soon I will have lilies in yellow, orange, and red blooming around it."

Maggie admired the globe from the porch. "It's amazing how the glass reflects the whole side yard. You can even see the bluebird box."

"That's exactly why I put it there. I can just sit here on my porch and enjoy the bluebirds sitting on top of their wooden box and not disturb them a bit."

While the pair talked about the gazing globe, Abby stared wide-eyed at Jean and smiled. Jean said, "Abby sure thinks I'm funny. That's another thing that happens when people get old. Their brains work on the same wavelength as a baby's. That's why old people and babies get along so well. They understand each other."

Maggie shook her head and smiled, "Jean, you crack me up."

"Maggie, I crack myself up."

The three went inside the house. Maggie put the muffins on the dining room table and then set up the play mat and play center. Abby was content to look at herself in the mirror and try to grab the rings at the top of the set. Jean had the table set using the antique teacups. She chose a different pair this time and had delicate dessert plates in place for the treats. Jean said, "Please, Maggie have a seat."

"Thank you. You do such a beautiful job setting the table. I feel so special coming over here."

"Special place settings for a special guest. It's not everyone who gets to feed the bluebirds in my yard."

"I hope I get to see them. I've never seen an eastern bluebird before."

"That reminds me, you know the gazing globe in the garden? It was originally used as what was called a silent butler. The glass balls used to sit on the tables of the very wealthy so the waitstaff could see from a distance who needed a glass filled or their plate cleared. It's a true antique and worth a bit of money. I can see you really love that gazing globe. When I die, I would like for you to have it. If I have my way, it will be yours before next winter because I really don't think I can stand another snowstorm."

"Jean. Don't say that."

"It's the truth, dear. One day when you look out your window and see the coroner's van sitting in front of my house, as soon as they pull away, you just walk your sweet little self over to my yard and carry the gazing globe back with you. From what I can remember of your house, there are plenty of places the globe would be perfect."

"Thanks, Jean, but can we talk about something else? I really like having you around."

"Maggie, I want you to have that gazing globe. Promise me you will take it."

"I promise."

"Thank you, dear. Okay, enough of that talk. You want to know about the neighborhood. This was a special place to live, still is. There were eight of us. Well, seven at first. One of us gorgeous young women was single for a while. Boy, did that cause some problems."

"Really? I thought you were all close friends."

"We were, but there were some problems here and there. Angie being single was one of them."

"Were a lot of women jealous of her?"

"Most were secure in their marriages. There was only one who had a problem with Angie."

"Who?"

"My friend who lived in your house."

"What is her name? Are you still friends with her?"

"Elizabeth is my friend's name and her husband is Eddie."

"So Eddie and Elizabeth. That's who used to live in our house. They sound good together."

"They were. They were a great couple. Eddie loved Elizabeth and there was no way that he had eyes for anyone else. Elizabeth just needed to realize that. Sometimes I don't think she was happy with the way her life turned out."

"What do you mean?"

"Well, I think she wanted a more glamorous life than what Eddie could offer."

"The parties in the front room sound pretty glamorous."

"They were, but Eddie liked to be at home. Elizabeth wanted to be whisked away here and there. She wanted to travel, but after the war, Eddie didn't really want to go anywhere far away. I can't blame him either. He was one of our heroic soldiers who stormed the beaches of Normandy. When he came back, Wyomissing Hills was his home and he didn't stray far from it."

"Where are Eddie and Elizabeth now?"

"They live in Arizona."

"Where are your other friends?"

"Everyone except for Marty and me eventually moved away. There was a tragic accident and after that nothing was ever the same again." Jean looked thoughtful for a moment, but her voice sounded calm and strong. Maggie wondered what happened and to whom.

"Is that one of the stories you're going to tell me?"

"Yes, but if I tell you the end of the story now, what would bring you back for another visit?"

"That I enjoy being with you." The baby started to fuss a little bit. They had been visiting for a little over an hour. Maggie didn't want to overstay her welcome, but she didn't want to go home yet either. She had to know about Jean and her friends, what their lives were like.

"Do you mind if I heat up Abby's bottle?"

"Please do. If you go now, what am I going to do with the rest of my day?"

"I was just thinking the same thing."

"Well then, that settles it. Get the bottle warmed up and let's go have a seat in the living room so you can get comfortable with Abby."

Maggie wrapped her infant in a blanket and cradled her in her arms as she ate. Maggie said, "So far I know a little bit about your friends Angie and Elizabeth and Eddie. There was also you and your husband, so there are two more, right?"

"Mike and Caroline were the last couple in our group of friends. They lived a few doors up from you to the left if you're facing your house."

Maggie could feel the excitement rise in her. She felt like a kid at story time, not knowing what Jean's words would bring next for the characters, but these weren't characters; these were real people and real lives.

As if sensing Maggie's thoughts, Jean said, "Why don't we begin with Elizabeth and Eddie?"

CHAPTER 6

When I was a small boy growing up in Kansas, a friend of mine and I went fishing and as we sat there in the warmth of a summer afternoon on a riverbank we talked about what we wanted to do when we grew up. I told him that I wanted to be a real major-league baseball player, a genuine professional like Honus Wagner. My friend said that he'd like to be President of the United States. Neither of us got our wish.

—*Dwight D. Eisenhower*

Eddie stepped up to the plate at Lauer's Park and focused on the cupola atop Deppen's Brewery just beyond the outfield. Eddie always eyed the cupola; it gave him something to aim for. The sound of the crowd behind him mixed together with one small voice standing out from among the others, "Come on, Eddie. Hit a homerun. Go Eddie." Eddie loved the sound of a kid yelling from the stands; he remembered his own youthful days cheering for his favorite players on the Reading Keys baseball team. As the pitcher set his stance, Eddie shifted his weight to his back leg. *Patience.* He was one of those rare players. A pitcher who could hit. Not every time, but enough of the time that other teams took his at-bat as a serious scoreboard threat. No pitcher wants his ERA foiled by another pitcher. Eddie watched the pitcher's eyes. *Inside fastball.* Even Eddie's sandlot buddies knew never to throw Eddie Getz an inside fastball. At just the right time, he pulled his hands in followed by a short, quick swing to ensure the sweet part of the bat would crush the ball. By the sound of the ball making contact with the bat, Eddie knew this one was gone. The noise happened simultaneously. The crack of the ball on the bat and the crowd erupting in cheers. As Eddie rounded the bases, he could still hear that one little voice, now more hoarse than before, "Yeah...Eddie...Yeah...Eddie." Eddie touched home plate with his right foot, and even if he had to do a little shuffle at the plate it was always his right foot, and ran toward the dugout. Eddie smiled to himself as he took a seat on the bench, but the cheer of the crowd begged for Eddie Getz to tip his hat. He was a shy man, but he knew how much that meant to the fans, so with a jog out of the dugout, he raised his hat over his head, waving at the filled grandstand.

Baseball. The one thing that Eddie loved. A standout in high school, he was picked up by the Reading team immediately after graduation. The news of his success in Reading traveled to the Philadelphia Phillies who were taking a close look at Eddie Getz. They liked what they saw and Eddie liked what he saw; a life in Philly baseball. But plans don't always go the way people think they will. It was in December of that year that America experienced, as Franklin D. Roosevelt described, "the day of infamy."

Eddie loved baseball, but he loved America more. Eddie traded his baseball uniform for an army uniform. Instead of going to Philadelphia to be a pitcher, he went to Kentucky for basic training. Instead of standing by a fence signing autographs, Eddie stood at attention in the ranks. The roar of the crowd was exchanged for the roar of the engines of fighter planes. Eddie's plans of being a major league base-ball player faded and when the war ended, his days on the mound were a distant memory.

The night before Eddie left for overseas, his friends took him out for one last night together. He looked forward to a good time that evening, but what he didn't know was that he would also meet the woman who would help him get through the war, the woman who would become his wife.

Elizabeth sat at the table in the middle of the pub. She wore a black dress, patent leather high heels and red lipstick. Her dark brown hair was pinned back in loose curls. Her best friend, Suzy, sat across from her. Elizabeth and Suzy attracted attention wherever they went. By contrast, Suzy had blond hair and blue eyes. Both women were stunning in their own way, but as soon as Eddie saw Elizabeth, he couldn't look at any other woman.

Elizabeth turned to Suzy, "Do you see that guy staring over here?"

"What about him?"

"He looks familiar. I swear we've seen him before."

"Mmm, he's very good-looking. We would remember."

Elizabeth studied Eddie as he continued to look at her, trying to recall his face. The bartender called to Eddie and he turned his head to look over his left shoulder. *That's it,* she thought as she remembered that exact turn of his head toward first base when he was standing on the mound.

Elizabeth stood up. "That's Eddie Getz, the Reading pitcher."

Although Eddie was too shy, even surrounded by his friends, to approach Elizabeth, he didn't need to; she was as forward as they come. The girls made their way over to the bar, Elizabeth getting to Eddie first, resting her right arm on the edge. "Are you going to buy me a drink or just stare at me all night?"

Now that Elizabeth had made the first move, Eddie's shyness fell away. "I'm going to buy you a drink, and if you don't mind, I'll keep staring as well."

"Good."

Elizabeth glanced behind her. One of Eddie's friends ordered a drink for Suzy, and on the surface she seemed taken by his charm, but underneath Suzy seethed at the thought of Eddie Getz paying attention to her friend. Men always looked at both of them, and then the girls would make their choice of which man interested them. Suzy was a little put off by Elizabeth's apparent lack of regard for her. *How dare she choose Eddie.*

Elizabeth turned her attention back to Eddie. "So what do you do?"

"Just got back from basic training. I made a short stop home before heading overseas."

It wasn't the answer Elizabeth was expecting from a promising ball player, but she maintained her poise, "Well, soldier. Do you need someone to write to you?"

"You bet. I'd be the luckiest soldier in the war to have the most beautiful girl in the States writing to me. You wouldn't happen to have a picture on you, would you? For proof, you know."

"I'll tell you what. After I receive your first letter, I'll send a picture that will make you the envy of your company."

Eddie found an outlet for the severity of the war in writing to Elizabeth. He was surprised how open and honest he could be through his writing. Several weeks after their encounter, Elizabeth received Eddie's first letter.

Dear Elizabeth,

As promised, I am writing to you. We just arrived here in England after a long and difficult trip. I bet this would be a beautiful place to visit after the war, and I would sure rather be here with you and in different circumstances.

Since the night we met, I haven't stopped thinking about you. I wish we could have had more time together before I left, but for now what little time we had will just have to suffice. I can't wait to learn all about you. What your life has been like up to this point and now what your plans are for the future. Tell me all about home and how the war is affecting people there. It's a terrible time in the world. We lost so many men in the attack on Pearl Harbor. By the end of the war, who knows how many men will be lost. So far we're waiting here until we get our orders to move. It is a stressful time for all of us. I don't want to say anything in this letter. Maybe sometime we will be able to talk face to face. I look forward to hearing from you. I hope you are well.

Eddie

Elizabeth put the letter on top of the desk knowing she would read it again and again. Keeping her word, she selected a picture of herself standing in her yard in a black one-piece bathing suit. Elizabeth thought a long time about what to write. They were both posturing the night they met, so the sincere and almost sad tone to Eddie's letter came as a surprise to her. She had no idea what Eddie must be going through, and she wanted to send words of healing, but she was stuck.

Suzy stopped by the day Elizabeth received Eddie's first letter. "What are you doing? Do you want to go out? There's a dance tonight at Jake's."

"I can't believe I'm going to say this, but no. I think I want to stay in and write back to Eddie."

Suzy's ears perked up, "You're writing to Eddie. The baseball player?"

"Yes. Can you believe it? He sent me such a wonderful letter."

"Let me see."

"Sorry, Suzy. It's a personal letter. Do you want something to drink before the dance? I have some fresh lemonade in the kitchen."

"That sounds wonderful."

As soon as Elizabeth left the room, Suzy picked up Eddie's letter. She skimmed the contents of the letter and then looked at the return address on the envelope. Suzy grabbed a pen from the desk and quickly wrote Eddie's address on her arm. She was just pulling her dress sleeve over the ink when Elizabeth walked into the room.

"Here you go, Suzy. We can sit and have a nice chat."

Suzy took the lemonade, careful not to extend her arm so much that the sleeve would creep up. The two women sat looking at each other for the first time in three years with nothing to say. Elizabeth broke the silence.

"Are you meeting anyone at the dance?

"Not really, although I'm sure I will know people there."

"Yes, well that's good. I'm sorry I'm not going. I just really want to get this letter finished."

Suzy drank her lemonade and smiled between sips. Once the glass was empty, she put it on the desk and stood to go. "Thank you, Elizabeth. Have a good evening."

"You do the same, Suzy."

You can count on it, she thought, as she got in her car and drove straight home. Sitting in her bedroom, Suzy took out a pen and paper. *My Dearest Eddie*, she wrote. Once Suzy finished the letter, she addressed the envelope, put a stamp in the corner, put it in the mail and thought, *We'll just see who Eddie Getz is really interested in.*

When Eddie heard his name called for mail, he jumped up from his seat and opened the letter without looking at the return address.

My Dearest Eddie,

I hope my letter finds you well. I think about you all the time. I wish we would have had time to talk the night before you left, but Elizabeth got to you first…

Eddie stopped reading and turned the letter over. *Suzy.* She must be the one who was at the bar with Elizabeth the night before his deployment. Why would she be writing to him and where did she get his address? Eddie slipped the letter back into the envelope without reading the rest of it. Eddie's name was called again and hope replaced his confusion. As soon as he opened the letter, the picture Elizabeth promised fell onto his lap. She was even more beautiful than Eddie remembered. He sat down on a crate slowly reading the letter from Elizabeth, savoring every word.

Dear Eddie,

Receiving your letter made me so happy. To hear you are doing well made me feel relieved. Thank you for sharing your experiences with me and please know that you can tell me anything you want. I'm a strong woman, and I can handle knowing what you are going through. I know we don't know much about each other, so I thought I would tell you a little about my life. I live on a farm—you probably didn't peg me for a farm girl. Believe me, I've been trying to rid myself of that kind of life for a while now. I decided to get myself a job. I'm working for a hat company. It's perfect for me. Right now, I'm one of the secretaries. I like it and the other girls sure are nice. I make a nice wage and I will be getting my own apartment as soon as I save up enough money. It should

only take me about two months to save. I hope when you
come home, we can spend some time together. It is strange
that I can miss someone I don't even know that well, but I do
miss you Eddie. Things would be so much easier if you were
here. I'm keeping busy with my job and with looking for an
apartment. I hope you are okay. Write to me when you can,
but I understand you might not be able to. Please know that I
am thinking about you.

Elizabeth

One of his fellow soldiers noticed the smile on Eddie's face and said, "A letter from your girlfriend."

"A letter and a picture."

The other men ran over. "Let us see."

Eddie beamed as they looked at the picture of Elizabeth. Some men whistled and some men asked, "How do I get a girl like that?"

Eddie felt lucky to have Elizabeth to, in some way, call his own. He had always been so shy, but baseball opened a whole new world to Eddie, one where the women approached him. Having Elizabeth stand by him while he was at war showed him she was a loyal woman. From her first letter, Eddie knew he would ask her to marry him when he returned.

During the two years that Eddie was at war, Elizabeth found the apartment she wanted. She had been able to afford nice furniture and kept her place clean and uncluttered.

When the marketing director for the hat company took one look at Elizabeth, he decided to promote her from secretary to his advertising model. She was even chosen to model for posters and billboards supporting the troops and the war effort. Life was going well for Elizabeth, but she wondered how Eddie would like the changes in her and she wondered if she would like the changes in him.

Over the passing months and years Eddie's letters had grown more serious in tone. He wrote more and more about the terrible time they were having. Eddie never went into detail, instead he wrote in generalities, but Elizabeth could tell something was different. She hoped that when Eddie returned, he would be able to get some semblance of his old self back. The change pained her. Before they met, Elizabeth went to many baseball games and she took the abundant time she had alone to recall Eddie as a ball player. He was confident on the mound and was a fan favorite. There had been an easiness to Eddie, but now there was a heaviness about him. In the last letter, he gave Elizabeth his arrival time in New York City and asked her to meet him there. *Elizabeth, my darling, you are the first person I want to see when I get back to the States. Meet me in New York.*

Elizabeth's job as a model took her to New York City on several occasions. The energy of the city was a long way from the quiet life she was used to as a farm girl. Elizabeth's time in New York was all business and left in her a desire to go back and enjoy the sights of the city. Eddie's return gave her the opportunity. She made reservations at the Edison Hotel, a place for them to spend some time getting to know each other and getting to know New York City. Elizabeth was nervous about the trip and wished she and Suzy were still close so that she could come along and perhaps make the meeting more comfortable, but the last two years took a toll on the two friends. Elizabeth wasn't sure what happened to their friendship, but she suspected it had something to do with Eddie. She sensed that Suzy was not entirely happy for her. They grew distant and the discord made Elizabeth uncomfortable and finally they just stopped talking. What Elizabeth didn't know is that Suzy wrote to Eddie every week. Eddie never read any of her letters; he didn't even open the envelope, except for the first one.

CHAPTER 7

Maybe all one can do is hope to end up with the right regrets.
—Arthur Miller

Jean took a sip of her coffee. "Eddie and Elizabeth eventually married, but Eddie made some choices that caused a strain in their relationship. One was throwing each of Suzy's letters in his bag instead of throwing them away. Another was turning down his second chance at baseball when the Phillies knocked on his door after he returned from the war."

Maggie couldn't keep quiet any longer. She had so many questions. "Eddie had the chance to be a major league ballplayer even after the war?"

"Yes he did. I was looking out my window one morning when a fancy car pulled up in front of our house. Two men dressed in suits got out and stood looking up at your house. At first I thought it might be bad news, but then Eddie and Elizabeth met the men on the front porch and Elizabeth's smile got bigger and bigger the longer they talked. I knew it was good news and I hoped it had something to do with baseball. Elizabeth always believed in Eddie's talent and when he came back from the war she thought maybe fulfilling his dream of being a pitcher would help him deal with the after-effects of the war, but he turned down the chance."

"Why did he turn it down?"

"He said that he had a job now and was ready to start a family. To take the chance of losing everything because he was chasing this dream just wasn't worth it. The sad thing is though, it was actually because he didn't take the chance that he almost lost everything. I don't even think the men were all the way down the block before Elizabeth starting yelling, 'Are you crazy? You are ruining your chances. This is your big break—you can't blow it.' I couldn't hear what Eddie said back to Elizabeth because he wasn't a yeller and remember I was in my house listening at the window, but Elizabeth told me later that Eddie liked the normalcy and calmness of an everyday job. He knew what to expect and there were never any surprises. He had had enough of those during the war."

"What happened to their marriage after Eddie made that decision?"

"It took a while for Elizabeth to let go of the bitterness. She really felt like they would have had a different life if he had become a major league pitcher. And she was right. Their life would have been a lot different, but they had a good life. Sure it had some bumps along the way, but all marriages do."

"Was one of the bumps when Elizabeth found the letters from Suzy?"

"Yes. That was a scene. Once again I was at my window and well, one day I see Elizabeth throwing envelopes out of her bedroom window; there must have been a hundred of them. And after the envelopes came Eddie's clothes."

"No."

"Yes. Eddie had really nice clothing and all of it was spread out on the front lawn for all the neighbors to see."

"What happened next?"

"The entire neighborhood could hear Elizabeth yelling. It took her a long time to warm up to Eddie again, but he loved her and was more patient than most men would have been. I mean the silent treatment Elizabeth gave Eddie was like none I've ever seen, poor guy."

As soon as Jean mentioned the silent treatment, Maggie felt convicted. It was as though she was getting a glimpse into her own life. Suddenly came the realization that she felt bad for Eddie with the way Elizabeth treated him, but here she was really doing the same thing to Scott. *I'm just like Elizabeth,* Maggie thought. She questioned why she hung on to this terrible way of relating to Scott. It wasn't healthy.

Jean sensed Maggie's distraction. "Are you okay, dear?"

"Oh. Yes, I'm sorry Jean. I just feel terrible for their marriage. It's obvious that Eddie loved Elizabeth and she just wouldn't embrace it. He never even opened the other letters from Suzy so there was nothing between them and the Phillies were a great opportunity, but I think he just wanted his family and an every-day kind of life, like you said. How many women would give up everything for a man who just wanted to love her and their family? Is this the sad part of the story you were talking about earlier?"

"It's a sad part, but it's not *the* sad part. Eddie and Elizabeth were okay after all that. They had two kids, a boy and a girl. Eddie coached his son in baseball and he got such enjoyment out of it. Eddie said teaching his son to pitch was better than standing on the mound himself. Their son became a major league pitcher. They were proud as punch. Eddie was a very stable man and he gave his family a stable life and a good life at that."

"What did their daughter do?"

"Oh, this is ironic. I love this part. She married a farmer."

"No."

"So here was Elizabeth as a young girl trying to escape the farmer's life and she finds herself as a middle-aged woman at her daughter's house all the time trying to help her become a farmer's wife."

"Was Elizabeth's daughter happy?"

"Yes. They were all happy. Elizabeth and Eddie, too."

"So ours is a happy home?"

"Yes, dear. It's all there within those four walls—laughter, joy, love, peace."

Maggie responded thoughtfully. "That's good to know."

"I guess you should be getting back to your handsome husband. Do you have dinner planned?"

Sometimes Maggie got the feeling that Jean knew about the problems in her marriage. Sometimes she felt like her house must be made of glass and Jean saw everything. If she really were transparent, Maggie didn't want to outright lie, so she said in a quiet voice, "I didn't plan dinner for tonight."

Jean took away any feeling of condemnation for her. "That's understandable, dear. You're a new mom and it takes some time to get used to handling so much. Maybe your handsome husband can take you and Abby out for a nice dinner. Have you explored the area yet?"

"No."

"Why don't I write down the name and address of a nice restaurant and you and your family can just have a relaxing night together. It's always nice when someone else takes care of doing the dishes."

Maggie wanted to explode and confess everything to Jean, to ask for some help and some guidance, but she was too embarrassed, so she kept silent about all her problems and instead smiled and said, "That sounds lovely. Thanks."

Maggie waited while Jean wrote down the restaurant's information.

As Jean handed the paper over, she asked "Do you know how to cook, dear?"

Maggie laughed a little and said, "Probably not as good as you."

"Do you have plans tomorrow?"

"I never have any plans."

"Then I want you to go to the store and buy these items. I'm going to teach you how to make a good dinner for your husband."

Jean had this way about her that made it difficult to say no. And besides, if Maggie said no, there would be questions to follow. Maggie simply replied, "You're in for a challenge teaching me how to cook."

"I'm up for it. It's been a while since I've had a good challenge in life. See you and Abby tomorrow and have a wonderful time at dinner this evening."

CHAPTER 8

Each one of us here today will at one time in our lives
look upon a loved one who is in need and ask
the same question: We are willing to help, Lord,
but what, if anything, is needed? For it is true
we can seldom help those closest to us.
Either we don't know what part of ourselves to give or,
more often than not, the part we have to give is not wanted.
And so it is those we live with and should know
who elude us. But we can still love them—we can love
completely without complete understanding.

—Norman Maclean, A River Runs Through It

On the walk back to her house, Maggie rehearsed what she would say to Scott. It had been so long since she had anything of value to say to him. Maggie dug deep within herself and brought to mind the day they first met. She was saddling up the horses getting them ready for the next scheduled tour. Her boss came over to her and said, "We have four guys we're taking out, so we just need one more horse and we'll be good to go." Maggie loved her job, sharing the history of Glacier National Park by showing people some of the off-the-main-trail places that most people don't get to on foot. She felt like she was getting paid to be a cowgirl.

As Maggie led the horses to the entrance gate, she observed the group. All guys her age. As soon as she saw Scott, she felt a smile spreading across her face and a warming in her heart. The guys were joking around with one another but quieted as Maggie and her boss approached. Maggie's boss always assigned the horses, and when he assigned her favorite horse, Whiskey, to Scott, he turned to his friend and said, "Hey, Derek. I think I was given your horse."

Thinking back to a few nights ago when maybe he did have a little too much to drink, Derek replied with a hint of sarcasm, "Good one, Scott."

Maggie smiled at the banter between the friends as they began their trek through the woods. Her job was to stay in the back and help anyone who seemed to be having trouble. This gave her the perfect view of Scott and she found herself admiring the way his crisp white t-shirt fit the curve of his shoulders and back. He was wearing boots and a cowboy hat and his brown hair showed only slightly underneath. He was probably the cutest guy she had ever seen. Scott glanced back at Maggie, catching her eye a few times during the trip. The trip lasted for two hours, and Maggie was sorry when it came to an end. She had wanted to talk to Scott along the trail, but the group had paid for a tour and that's what they got. Besides, Maggie didn't exactly take this job so she could find a boyfriend. She watched as the group of friends walked toward the parking lot and jumped into a red Jeep Wrangler. The dust that kicked up from the tires obscured her view as Scott and his friends drove away. Maggie didn't think she would ever see Scott again until the next morning when the first group of people gathered for a tour. There was an older married couple and Scott. He was given a different horse for this tour, Chestnut. She was a good horse, very calm. This time Scott lagged in the back with Maggie, bringing his horse aside of hers.

"I hope you don't think I'm weird for coming back again, but I really wanted to get a chance to talk to you."

Maggie held back her excitement. She thought she had lost her chance with Scott. "I don't think you're weird. I actually think it's kind of nice you came back again."

"*Really?* Well, in that case, can I tell you that you are the most beautiful girl I've ever seen and I would love to take you to dinner tonight?"

That memory of Scott made it easier for Maggie to approach her husband. He opened the front door and met her halfway up the walkway. "Why don't you take Abby into the house, and I'll get the stroller."

"Thanks." Maggie watched as Scott folded up the stroller. When he turned around, she was still looking at him.

Scott was taken aback a bit. His wife rarely looked at him these days. "Are you ready to go in?"

"Yes, but first, I didn't make dinner." *Not that I ever made dinner anymore,* Maggie thought. *What a dumb thing to say.* "Jean gave me an idea for a restaurant the three of us could go to. I thought maybe we could go tonight."

"That sounds great, Maggie. What restaurant?"

Maggie hadn't looked at the piece of paper, but she pulled it out of her pocket and said, "Well, that's interesting."

"Oh really? Where are we going?"

"The Hitching Post."

Before Maggie could change her mind, Scott put Abby's diaper bag over his shoulder and placed her in her car seat. It was a short fifteen-minute drive to the restaurant. Maggie asked Scott about his day, something she hadn't done in a while. It was nice to have a conversation with his wife. He missed this about the two of them, the ease they once had with each other. When they got to the restaurant, the sign for The Hitching Post had a rope around the "H" as though it had been rounded up. On the old barn-wood walls inside the restaurant hung paintings of horses. Maggie felt like she was back in Montana. For a moment she sensed a little pang of remembrance but tried not to let it take over her and the night. She was going to try to get the life back that she had always wanted and to do that she had to move forward.

The hostess showed them to their table and shared the specials for the evening. After she said, "Your waitress will be with you shortly" and walked away, Scott turned to Maggie, "Jean certainly knew what she was doing sending a cowgirl to a place like this."

Maggie smiled. "I was thinking the same thing. You were a pretty good cowboy yourself."

"Thanks, but I feel like the fly-fisherman role suited me better."

"There is definitely something romantic about a fly-fisherman in Montana."

"I think that's a notion from Brad Pitt's character in *A River Runs Through It.*"

Maggie felt a surge of happiness talking about the memories they shared from their early years together. "No, it was definitely you who made it romantic. You were very patient with me when you taught me to cast a line. I always enjoyed that in you, your patience." Maggie thought about how much Scott had put up with from her these past few months. Most men would have given up, maybe even sent her back to Montana.

Scott was surprised by the change in Maggie. He was happy to have his wife back and as she talked about the stories Jean told her earlier in the day, he listened intently not knowing how long this change in his wife would last, but he hoped it was for good.

On the way home Maggie said, "Oh. I almost forgot. Jean is teaching me how to make an Italian dish tomorrow. Can we stop at the food store before we go home? I need to get some ingredients."

"Sure," Scott said as he thought, *I don't know what Jean is up to, but she just might be the wisest person I know.*

CHAPTER 9

The bird, a nest; the spider, a web; man, friendship.
— William Blake

Maggie and Jean planned for an early afternoon cooking session. Maggie spent the morning cleaning up around the house and taking Abby for a long walk around the neighborhood. The air was still crisp, but the sun felt warm on Maggie's face. The nicer weather drew people outside and along the route many small children played in their yards. Some were on swing sets, some sat on driveways with toy trucks or sidewalk chalk.

The elementary school was located in the neighborhood. There were two parks and a nice pool for the residents. Maggie had spent some evenings reading over the welcome booklet for Wyomissing Hills: there were Memorial Day and Fourth of July parades and at Christmas there was a light decorating contest and luminary display. With the community's focus on the family, this certainly seemed like the ideal place to raise kids, but Maggie still missed home.

At one o'clock Maggie packed a grocery bag with the mild Italian sausage and parsley, red peppers, pappardelle pasta, and beef broth before heading across the street.

Jean sat on her front porch waiting for a day of cooking and friendship. She watched as the bluebirds sat atop the gazing globe unaware of her presence. When she saw Maggie approaching with the stroller, she got up to greet her while pressing her finger to her lips and quietly saying, "Shhhh, come and see the bluebirds."

Maggie gently picked up Abby and the three tiptoed to the end of the porch. "There they are."

Maggie smiled. "They are so beautiful. What a special surprise. Do you see the birds?" Abby smiled and pointed. Jean smiled while watching Maggie and Abby enjoy the bluebirds. She thought, *Maggie is such a good mom, she just needs to hang in there and work through this difficult time.* Once the bluebirds flew away, Jean said, "What a wonderful treat that was. Abby, is this your first bluebird?"

Maggie nodded. "It's a first for both of us." Reaching under the stroller, she grabbed the bag from the storage area underneath. "I have all the ingredients. I think Scott is looking forward to dinner tonight."

"And how was your dinner last night?"

"Oh, it was so nice. I mean The Hitching Post. I felt like I was back in Montana. The paintings of the horses reminded me of the ones I used to ride."

"I thought that might be a nice place for a handsome cowboy to take his cowgirl."

"I told Scott that he makes a good cowboy, but he sees himself as more of a fly fisherman."

"Yes, I recall you mentioned that was his summer job."

"You have quite the memory, Jean. I don't even remember telling you that."

"That's because you have a whole lot more to think about than I do, dear. Now let's get this dinner together."

Jean sat in the dining room holding Abby and directing Maggie. While the pasta boiled, she cut the sausage into little pieces and sautéed them in a pan as she sliced the red peppers and chopped the parsley. Once the sausage browned, Maggie added the red peppers and beef broth. She let that simmer on low and then tossed in the pasta and parsley. Maggie looked forward to dinner tonight. "Jean, this smells so good. I can hardly wait to eat. Why don't you come to my house and have dinner with us?"

"No, dear. I want to be at home."

"Well, then, why don't we eat here with you?"

"Maggie, I'm fine. I get tired and need some time to rest."

"I feel bad that you're going to eat dinner by yourself and we are right across the street and we're having dinner together. That makes me sad, Jean."

"It makes me glad, sweetie. You're a young family. You should be having dinner together. Listen, I hardly eat anything anymore. Looking up at your house, seeing the lights lit, knowing you're there with your husband and daughter; that makes me happy. It makes me feel peaceful and safe, so don't you worry about me, dear. I'm exactly where I want to be."

There was no sense in arguing with Jean. She was stubborn, and besides, Maggie knew she loved being in her house surrounded by all of the things that brought back memories of her husband and kids. Maggie put the dinner in containers and placed them on a shelf in the refrigerator. Abby started to fuss a bit.

"I think sweet pea is hungry. I can still hold her if you want to warm the bottle."

Maggie dug the bottle out of the diaper bag and heated it in the kitchen. Jean seemed to enjoy holding a baby. Maggie asked, "Would you like to give Abby her bottle?"

"Oh. It's been a long time since I've done that." Jean looked down at the baby and then back up at Maggie. "Yes, I would love to give Abby her bottle, but take her while I walk over to the sofa. It will be more comfortable for all of us and I am in no shape to be carrying a baby around."

Once her friend was situated, Maggie placed the infant in Jean's arms and handed her the bottle. As Abby drank from the bottle, she studied this woman who was holding her and lifted her little hand and wrapped her fist around Jean's fingers. "She is so precious, Maggie." Delighting in every minute of cradling the baby in her arms, Jean didn't take her eyes off Abby's delicate face. The two women sat silently on the sofa, letting this moment do for their friendship what words never could.

CHAPTER 10

Life would be infinitely happier if we could only
be born at the age of eighty
and gradually approach eighteen.

–Mark Twain

Several days had gone by since Maggie's cooking session with Jean. Scott loved the dinner, and Maggie loved it too. It was their new favorite meal. Maggie was eager to learn more and took to researching recipes on the Internet. Things were better between them. She was trying hard although their marriage wasn't close to where it used to be or where it should be.

The early days of April saw temperatures in the 70s and Maggie thought it would be a good time to get Jean out of the house, so she invited her to a picnic in the park at the very spot the horse show used to take place. Jean dressed in black slacks and a cream-colored sweater. She wore pearls around her neck and black patent flats. *Jean always has herself put together,* Maggie thought.

Once at the park, Jean needed to use her cane to walk to the location of the horse show marker. Maggie read the plaque aloud to Jean, "The Reading Horse Show was held at this site from the early 1930s until 1942. The riding competition was a charity event sponsored by the Junior League of Reading. In its prime, the two-day event drew hundreds of people. It was resurrected for a short time after the war, but the last show was held in 1949. Some of the horses in the show were boarded at the Goodman Barn. This is the Red barn on the left as you head out Old Wyomissing Road towards Ruth's Bridge."

"So this is where it all took place."

"This is where it all happened." Jean turned around and pointed to the barn. "That's the barn the plaque mentions."

"It's right across the street. Without you, Jean, I could have passed this place a million times and not known any of this."

Maggie could see how this would be a prime location for a horse show with its expansive, flat area. There was plenty of room for the riding course as well as a carnival. A stream and some benches were beyond the flat grassy area. Maggie pushed the stroller as the three made their way to one of the benches. They chose a nice spot in the sun. It was a comfortable temperature for a picnic—just enough sun to warm them and just enough of a breeze to keep them from getting too hot. Maggie unpacked the lunch—simple ham sandwiches on rye bread, fruit salad, homemade brownies, and water.

"Thank you for the lunch, Maggie."

"You're welcome. I hope you like it."

"I love it."

A family of ducks floated down the stream, so Maggie turned the stroller so that Abby could see them. "Look, honey. Ducks."

She pointed and laughed. Abby got louder as the ducks got closer, and they quickly headed to the other side of the stream, much to her dismay. That didn't stop her from trying to talk to the ducks, although no one but maybe Abby knew what she was saying.

"Abby makes me laugh. It's so nice to have a baby around again. They are such a delight. You are a good mom, Maggie."

"Thanks. Sometimes I don't feel like it though."

"You're a great mom. Why would you say that?"

"I feel like since our move from Montana, Abby is missing so much. She doesn't have any extended family here. Just Scott and me."

"That's all a child needs, dear."

"I just wanted so much more for Abby."

"Listen, a daughter needs a mom who delights in her. Delight in Abby all of her days and you will find yourself with a very happy daughter who possesses strength, peace, love, and compassion. Girls thrive when they know how much joy they bring to their mom."

"That's very insightful. I didn't find that piece of wisdom in any of the baby books I read."

"That's because I didn't write them."

"You know, Jean, I think you should write some books about life. I'm learning more from you than from anyone else I've ever met."

"After raising two boys, I do know a thing or two about being a parent."

Maggie wanted to learn as much as she could from Jean. She felt this woman in front of her held the key to all it meant to be a woman, a wife, and a mother.

"How do you know so much about raising a girl? You have boys and here you are telling me about what a girl needs."

"Boys. Girls. It's not that hard, Maggie. Look back over your life. What makes you happiest when you think of your mom?"

So many memories of her mom came to mind, but her happiest was when her mother took her to a friend's horse barn. "I had been talking about riding horses for so long. I just loved horses. I read every book about horses that I possibly could, watched *The Black Stallion* every chance I got. One day, my mom said she was taking me for a drive. We took some back roads and all of a sudden we pulled into a long driveway lined with trees and a split rail fence. I looked out the window and saw horses running through pastures on both sides of the property. My mom smiled and said, 'I don't think you've ever met my friend Sue.'" Maggie got a faraway look in her eyes and continued. "We pulled up to a barn and my mom's friend greeted us. I remember her, fitted jeans, black riding boots, a crisp white shirt. She waved and when my mom stopped the car, Sue ran to my mom and they hugged. I let myself out of our car and my mom met me half way and put her arm around me. Sue extended her hand. 'Maggie, you're all grown up. I haven't seen you since you were a baby.' Shaking hands is something my mom taught me to do from the time I was young, so I gave a nice, firm handshake. My mom seemed proud of me for that. Sue then led me into the stables and showed me the horses she boarded. She showed me three of her own horses and how to saddle them up. The three of us rode the trails on her property, through streams, over meadows, and finally back to the barn."

"That's a nice memory of your mom."

"It is and what's more is she knew this is where my heart was, with the horses. She got me lessons and I when I was old enough, I eventually got a job at Sue's barn and then finally at Glacier giving riding tours of the park. My mom was instrumental in all of that. She knew what joy being around horses gave me, and she has always been there for me."

"What a beautiful story about you and your mom. See how she delighted in you?"

"I do. She listened to me. And even though I would have done anything she wanted me to do, my mom gave me what made me happy."

"Yes, she did. And you know what? You're going to do the same thing for Abby, and that's going to be a true testament to what your mother did for you."

"You're right, Jean. You're always right about these things."

A smile spread across her friend's face.

"Well, what about you? How have you raised your sons and how do you handle that they now are both living in a different state?"

"Good question. I raised my boys to have the same character as my husband. Marty was a true man. He was secure in himself. He knew how to support a family. He loved and adored me and our boys followed in his footsteps with their own marriages. They always knew we would support them no matter what, but if they messed up, they would pay at home. Neither of the boys wanted to disappoint either one of us, so they were on their best behavior. Bobby and Johnny were both top athletes in high school. They played football and baseball. Marty and I had so much fun gathering with the neighbors at the stadium on a Friday night. Then we all took turns having a party at one of our houses afterward, the parents and the kids. I have so many good memories of those times that I cherish. Even all these years later, there's something about this place that makes it ideal for raising kids. Maybe it's the long tradition of community here. This is a place that was built for family. That's why there's so many different types of houses, some big, some small; so grandparents, parents, and children could buy houses near each other."

"Does it disappoint you that your boys moved away?"

"Not at all. Besides the sports, Bobby and Johnny loved racing as well. Every chance they got, Marty would have them at a race in the pit. They loved it and had such a great time. Johnny used his experience with motors and vehicles in the military. They were both experts with mechanics and NASA was a good fit for both of them. I'm glad they are together and that they're best friends. What a comfort to me that when I'm gone, they both still have each other."

Maggie wished Jean wouldn't talk that way. She hated thinking about Jean not being around anymore. "Well, you're the only one I have."

"You are sweet to say that, dear, but you have your husband. The two of you moved across the country. I'm sure there's still some adjusting to do, but that will come and you will make more friends here. Now, we still have a lot to talk about. What did you learn from the former residents of your house, Eddie and Elizabeth?"

"Wow. We're getting right into the thick of things here, are we?"

"Yes. When you get old, you don't have time to dilly-dally, dear."

"Okay, then. I learned our plans for our lives aren't always what come to fruition, but there's always something better."

"That's a good start."

"I'm sure more will come to me over time."

"How about I tell you about Angie and Frank?"

"I would love that. Which house was theirs again?"

"A few houses up on the same side as ours. I mean mine. I always do that. I think of the house as Marty's and mine, ours together even though he's been gone for so long. When you really love someone, they are always a part of your life, no matter what."

Jean sighed and seeing the tears welling in Maggie's eyes, hurried on with the story. "Angie became a nurse just prior to World War II, and after the attack on Pearl Harbor, she joined the Army Nurse Corps. Guess where she met Frank."

"The war?"

"Nope.

"The neighborhood?"

"No, but good guess."

Joking, Maggie said, "The circus?"

"Close."

CHAPTER 11

I may be compelled to face danger, but never fear it,
and while our soldiers can stand and fight,
I can stand and feed and nurse them.

— Clara Barton

Angie had a day off from the hospital on December 7 and had planned on meeting her friend Georgie, who was also a nurse at the hospital, for a movie at the Park Theater, which ran older movies and only cost ten cents. When the women left the theater at one o'clock that day, they reached the sunny sidewalk to shouts of "Nation at War. Get your special edition." Angie bought a newspaper and the headlines read, "It's War." Radio stations relayed information all day long directing citizens how they could be of service. Without hesitation and without any formal military training both young women signed up for the Army Nurse Corps. Their only request was for the two friends to serve together. They had gone through nursing school together and worked the same shift at the hospital. Angie and Georgie went into duty ignorant of military protocol, customs, defense tactics, and organization, but they went in together.

The night before they left for overseas, Angie prayed. *God, I don't know what is going to happen in this war, but please give me the strength and wisdom to help our soldiers and please never let their real condition show on my face.*

The pair found themselves heading for the Philippines on a transport to set up a hospital ahead of an American initiative.

"Angie, do you think we're prepared enough for this?"

"Not at all. I don't think we have any idea what we're really going to face."

"I have that same feeling."

"But we need to do this for our soldiers. We've had good medical training and that will kick in with our first patient."

"I'm kind of glad now that we had Dr. Harrington for a teacher."

"I never thought I'd hear you say that, Angie. Remember how we used to call him 'Dr. Harrassington?'"

"How could I forget? He harassed me more than anyone else. I could never do anything right in his eyes and he always called me out on it in front of everyone. It made me a better nurse, though."

"The best nurse. You became the best nurse in our class and I'm pretty sure Dr. Harrington knew your potential. That was his way of getting you to reach it."

"I could have done it with a few less embarrassing situations."

"Well, your embarrassing situations kept the rest of us on our toes. We didn't want to be in your shoes, so thank you."

"You're welcome. I'm glad I could be of service."

Angie and Georgie smiled at each other and then grew silent for a moment. Angie broke the silence again.

"I feel nervous and sick to my stomach."

"So do I. I think that's normal."

"I wonder what it's going to be like where we're going."

"Horrible. It's going to be horrible."

When the plane landed in a clearing, adrenaline took over. The group of doctors and nurses trudged through the thick ground cover. They wore helmets and carried packs like the soldiers, only their Red Cross armband distinguished them as a medical team. They were covered in sweat by the time they found the abandoned barracks where they were to set up. There were eighteen wooden cots that would serve as operating tables and beds. No one in the barrack hospital, nurses and doctors alike, had any idea what they were in for. They waited through the first day into the night without event. In the early morning hours of the next day that all changed; planes flew overhead, bombs exploded in the near distance, and machine gun fire seemed to go on incessantly. By mid-morning the concrete floor was covered in blood and men. Only those who had a chance to survive would get a bed. Angie went from man to man assessing their wounds. She talked with them, held their hands, let them hold onto her arm for comfort, but through all of it God answered her prayer and her face never gave away the severity of their injuries. As soldiers lay dying, they saw in Angie peace and light as she spoke words of comfort over them. By the end of the second day, the hospital was under fire. Georgie became so indignant over the hospital being attacked that it took everything Angie had to keep her from going outside. Their stay in the Philippines saw many casualties, and finally four months later they were evacuated to Australia. Only Angie and Georgie's transport made it safely. All other transports were intercepted by the enemy, and many of their fellow nurses were suddenly prisoners of war.

Undaunted and in honor of their imprisoned colleagues, Angie and Georgie continued their service in the Army Nurse Corps with their next assignment taking them to North Africa.

One night during their journey to North Africa, Georgie whispered to Angie, "Do you miss home?

"I haven't even thought about home."

"I think about home all the time. It's what has gotten me through all this so far. And you. I'm not sure what I would have done without you here."

"I'm glad we're together, too. Just think about the stories we'll have to tell our grandchildren."

"I never thought when we were in nursing school that our profession would carry us across the world."

"We're certainly getting to see the world, but in a much different way than most people. That's for sure."

"When the war is over, I want to travel to Italy. We could go together. Just take some time to have fun and get away from the memories of what we've seen."

"I'm all for that, Georgie."

"I want to see beautiful things. Michelangelo's *David* and the Sistine Chapel. I bet seeing them would make me forget about the things we've seen here."

"I imagine that would help."

"We could also sit by the Trevi Fountain and make wishes all day. What would you wish for?"

"That depends. How many do I get?"

"As many as you want."

"Then I would wish for the war to be over. I would wish for us to meet the most handsome men we've ever seen and have them fall deeply and madly in love with us. I would wish that we would have a double wedding."

"That all sounds good. I like the double wedding idea with the most handsome men in the world."

Angie looked over at one of the doctors. "I think he has his eye on you."

"Oh, stop it. Dr. Jamison? Really? What makes you say that?" Georgie turned and looked at the doctor. She whispered, "He is really, really cute."

"I've caught him looking at you. I think he might like you."

"Hmmm…I wonder if he's been to Italy."

Angie stifled a giggle. "Oh, Georgie. I don't know, but he seems to be the kind of guy who would take you to Italy regardless."

"He does look like that kind of guy, doesn't he? Don't worry, Angie. You could come along with us."

"Oh, please. I think I would be fine if you and Dr. Cutie Pie went on your own."

"I'm going to be keeping a lookout to see if I can catch one of his glances."

Less than a minute later, Dr. Jamison looked over his shoulder. When he saw Georgie looking at him, he turned around quickly but then looked again. Georgie never averted her eyes and this time when the doctor looked at her, he smiled. Georgie smiled back and said to Angie, "That didn't take long."

"No, it didn't." A smile spread across Angie's face that quickly turned into a giggle and soon both women held their hands over their mouths trying to muffle the laughter that threatened to erupt and break the silence of the group.

Dr. Jamison worked up the nerve to talk to Georgie the next day. "Hi, I'm Ben."

"Hi, Ben. My name is Georgia, but my friends call me Georgie."

"It's nice to meet you."

"Likewise."

"So where are you from?"

"Pennsylvania."

"Where about?"

"A small town about an hour and a half northwest of Philadelphia."

"What a coincidence. I'm from Philadelphia. Well, Georgie, what do you say that when we get back to the States, I take you out to a nice dinner?"

"I would love to have dinner with you."

"Do you like Italian?"

"As a matter of fact, I do."

The evening before their arrival in North Africa, Georgie said to Angie, "The first thing I'm going to do when we're out of here is find out if Dr. Cutie, I mean Ben, has a good-looking friend for you."

"Georgie, I will meet the right guy on my own terms. Maybe you should get to know Dr. Cutie, I mean Ben, before you start setting me up with his friends."

"When you're in wedded bliss, you might be thanking me one day."

"We'll see."

Once they landed, under the cover of night the medical team shimmied down the side of the ship into a transport boat. They brought along as many supplies as they could, holding their heavy packs above their heads as they waded through the water to shore. This time they were able to use a hospital that had been evacuated, but there was no electricity and the supplies had been pillaged so they only had what they carried in. The first day of battle, the hospital saw one hundred patients. The crew of doctors and nurses handled that number easily, but the next day saw two hundred more men. They were running out of supplies and the medical transport was two days behind. Angie and Georgie improvised any way they could. The doctors, especially Ben, admired their efficiency, ingenuity, and compassion.

The bombings of the hospital began shortly after the medical supply transport arrived. This time it was Angie who almost ran outside to wave her arms and scream, *This is a hospital, how dare you?* Both women had just finished assisting in an operation on a shrapnel wound on a soldier's leg. The next thing Georgie saw was Angie heading straight for the door. Georgie got to Angie before she could exit and said, "What do you think you're doing?"

"I've had enough of this bombing. We're a hospital. You don't bomb hospitals. I'm going to stop them."

"I know you're angry. I feel the same way, but you're nothing against those planes and they won't even be able to see you and if they do see you, well, then we have one less nurse on our staff and we need everyone we can get."

Angie pulled herself together. At some point in time each nurse felt the same about the attacks on the hospital, but they maintained their purpose and continued to minister to the injured. They served a short time in the hospital in North Africa, but nurses were also needed near the front lines. Angie and Georgie volunteered for these missions where they carried tents and medical supplies near the front lines to set up mobile hospitals.

On one of the missions, Georgie asked Angie, "Do you think we're going to make it?"

"We're going to make it Georgie, and you and Ben are going to get married and have kids and live a wonderful life together."

Angie and Georgie kept each other going through the hard times. When one seemed close to despair, the other stepped in with words of support and encouragement. They continued their work on the front lines. It was tiring and dangerous, but the two friends were committed to helping the soldiers.

From North Africa the two friends and the rest of their crew went to a town in Italy thirty miles south of Rome. Lack of troops and supplies and poor military strategy made this battle long and costly in lives. The need for experienced mobile units brought Angie and Georgie into intense fighting. The mobile hospital was under greater attack than ever before. The Red Cross sign hanging outside the tent made the mobile hospital a target instead of a safe haven for wounded and dying soldiers. Bombs went off around the tents and gunfire hit the ground outside. The doctors and nurses relished the short bursts of peace they were afforded and took that time to recoup their focus and their strength.

One night after a particularly difficult but successful surgery, Angie and Georgie went outside for some air. It wasn't really fresh air they were going out for since there was always a hint of smoke lingering; it was more to get into an open space away from all the blood and suffering and death. As the two women stood in silence, a plane engine broke through the quiet, and flying overhead, opened its gun turret, raining bullets down on the hospital. As they turned to run, a bullet struck Georgie in the back. She took a few steps and reached her arm out to Angie's shoulder. Angie turned and raised her voice over the chaos, "What's wrong? Are you hurt?"

Georgie muttered, "My back."

Angie put her arm around Georgie's waist and supported her weight as she tried to get the two of them to safety. Angie guided Georgie to a stack of wooden crates. She could feel the blood from the bullet wound seeping onto her arm. Angie helped Georgie to the ground, sat next to her friend, and put pressure on the wound.

Georgie said, "I know it's bad."

Angie's face never let on that her friend was dying. "It isn't bad. We're going to get you fixed up and in no time you and I are going to be traveling through Italy together. We're going to see Michelangelo's statue of David and we'll see his paintings and we'll toss coins into the Trevi Fountain all day long."

Georgie smiled up at Angie, and as she watched her talk and watched her face, all she saw was light. In the arms of her friend she felt comfort and peace as she drew her last breath. When the last bit of life was out of Georgie, Angie held her friend close to her and sobbed. Ben and another doctor ran toward Angie with a stretcher. When Ben saw Georgie, he said to Angie, "No. Please tell me no," and fell to his knees sobbing. As more planes began to fly overhead, the three carried Georgie's body to the mortuary tent and gently placed her on the ground.

Ben knelt beside Georgie and took her hand. "I was going to ask her to marry me. I was planning all of it out for when we got back home."

Angie's voice cracked. "She would have said yes."

Angie prayed over her friend. *God, I pray you have Georgie, that she is with you and she is laughing and dancing and rejoicing. Lord, give the rest of us the strength to continue our work. We pray You guide our hands and give us the wisdom to heal our soldiers. Amen.*

Angie covered Georgie with a sheet and then wiped the tears from her own eyes. Part of Angie never wanted to return to the hospital. She wanted to walk away and never come back to this place. Out of fear she would do just that, Angie quickly said, "We have work to do."

Ben didn't move. He kept looking at the form of the body under the sheet, half expecting Georgie to sit up. She was supposed to be his wife. He had it all planned out. The engagement ring. The proposal. Everything. This must be a dream and he waited hoping to wake up.

Angie repeated more sternly than she had intended. "Dr. Jamison. We have work to do."

Ben broke out of his trance and stood up. The doctors walked back to the surgical tent each on one side of Angie. She kept her eyes straight ahead and never looked down at her uniform stained with the blood of her best friend. The continued heavy shelling brought in so many casualties that Angie thought the influx would never end.

Patient after patient, it was Angie who maintained composure. As she assisted Ben in surgery, she saw him begin to shake. "Everything okay, Doctor?"

Ben looked at her for a second, but he gathered himself and the shaking stopped. He pushed the thought of Georgie out of his mind. They both did.

Angie continued to care for the soldiers. Some she was able to heal and some she could only comfort as they lay dying. Angie maintained all that a nurse should possess: inner beauty, strength, courage, and compassion.

When the war ended, Angie went back to America and to her old job at the hospital, pressing on day after day and week after week, dealing the best she could with the grief of losing her best friend.

A few months later as Angie walked out of the emergency room after an uneventful shift, she saw Ben waiting for her on a bench. Ben stood up when he saw Angie. All the emotion Angie had held in since Georgie's death came to the surface like a flood as she ran to Ben, throwing her arms around his neck and sobbing. They stood that way for a long time while people passed by wondering what kind of tragedy must have befallen them. Finally, they drew apart and Ben said, "Let's go for a drive."

They remained silent until they came to a park a few minutes from the hospital.

Ben started the conversation. "I can't stop thinking about Georgie. I feel like I can't move on with my life and that I'll never have any semblance of normalcy ever."

"I feel that way, too. I just don't understand. Why Georgie? I keep asking myself, why did we go outside that day at exactly that time? If we had just stayed inside, Georgie would still be alive."

"It was the enemy who killed Georgie. The hospital never should have been under attack. All of us did the best we could and sometimes the only way to get some relief was to go outside away from all the suffering."

"I just wish there was just one morning that I didn't wake up and the first image I see is Georgie dead in my arms. I feel like I'm going crazy sometimes."

"Sometimes I think I am already crazy. Oh, Angie. I don't know what to do anymore."

"I guess all we can do is the best we possibly can, help as many people as we can."

A few boys had gathered in the park to play a game of baseball. Angie and Ben watched the first inning of the pick-up game in silence. At the top of the second inning Ben finally said, "Do you remember when life was that simple?"

"No, I don't."

He shook his head. "I don't either."

Ben drove Angie back to her apartment. Before she got out of the car Ben offered, "Any time you need anything, to talk or anything, please call me."

He handed her a small piece of paper with his number.

"Thank you, Ben. Take care."

Once inside her apartment, Angie crumbled up the piece of paper and threw it away.

CHAPTER 12

There is a wisdom of the head,
and there is a wisdom of the heart.

– Charles Dickens

T hat's a sad story."

"It is."

"Did Angie ever see Ben again?"

"No, they never saw each other again, but Ben did call Angie every once in a while to check in with her. There was a bond between the two of them, but it was a tragic bond. I think after a while it became too painful for them to have any contact with one another."

"It's such a terrible experience. I don't know how anyone overcomes something like that."

"Angie used that experience to make her an even better nurse after the war. She became the head nurse in the emergency unit at the hospital. She was strong, but sometimes she also seemed lost."

"I learned about World War II in history books, but I never heard stories like the ones you tell. I would have paid much more attention if we had learned more than just dates and names of battles. There were never any lives put with the facts. This is all so fascinating to learn."

"It was a fascinating time. Suddenly the whole country was one, all acting together for a common purpose. The attack on Pearl Harbor was a shock. We listened to the radio nonstop. It's not like now where you have the Internet and these phones that everyone is carrying around. The only pictures we had were in the newspapers. Now, you have up-to-the-second news. We anticipated what would happen next and sometimes it took until the next day before we knew what was happening in the world. Now you can get up in the middle of the night and know."

"It's interesting to think about a time before the information age."

"The World War II era was a time of wisdom. Today we have a ton of information, more information than we know what to do with, but what's really lacking is wisdom."

"I could use a little of that wisdom now."

"Why do you say that?"

"Last night Scott asked me to go to a party for the colleagues in his department at the college next weekend. I didn't go to the president's party, so I feel like I need to attend this one. I don't know who would watch Abby and I'm not comfortable leaving her right now."

"Oh, honey, I wish I could watch Abby for you but I'm in no shape to take care of a baby. She is your precious little daughter. You leave her when you feel comfortable and with whom you feel comfortable. Perhaps get to know some people in the neighborhood or maybe people Scott works with. There's a young girl down the street, Ellen. She's sixteen going on thirty, very mature and responsible. You could call her and see how she and Abby get along."

"Maybe I'll try that. Thanks, Jean."

On their way home Jean said, "It was so nice to get out of the house and sit in the park for a while. Thank you so much for such a nice day. I'm ready for a nap."

Maggie glanced in the rearview mirror at Abby who had fallen asleep in her car seat. "It looks like someone beat you to it."

CHAPTER 13

The single biggest problem with communication
is the illusion that it has taken place.

− *George Bernard Shaw*

Once at home, Maggie found Ellen's number and called. Ellen seemed excited to be given the opportunity to watch a baby and showed up at the front door the next day five minutes before the scheduled time. She gently knocked on the front door and spoke in a hushed tone as she entered the house. Ellen's care with not making noise impressed Maggie as did the list of recommendations she brought along with her.

Maggie showed the potential new sitter into the great room in the back of the house where Abby sat in her bouncy seat. She even remembered the baby's name from the discussion the night before. "Hi, Abby."

Ellen got right down on the floor in front of Abby and began playing and talking to her. Abby handed little toys to Ellen, who took them and acted like the blocks and caramel-colored stuffed dog were the most important things in the world. Maggie felt herself smile as she watched the two of them. It seemed she wasn't going to be able to use not having a babysitter as an excuse not to go out with her husband anymore.

Maggie was starting to feel better about her life in Pennsylvania, and although she felt a little nervous about leaving Abby, she was actually looking forward to the party with Scott. In Montana, they had been such a close couple and Maggie only ever saw happiness for them and their future, until this move across the country.

Maggie chose her party ensemble carefully, a simple but fitted black dress with patent leather black pumps. She let her hair fall straight, framing her face. Maggie wanted Scott to find her attractive, especially since her behavior had been less than that over the past few months, and even though she was a beautiful woman, her inner struggles since the move left her feeling less than great about herself. Tonight would be the start of a new life for them. They would put Montana behind them and focus on their life as a family in their new home, Pennsylvania. It would be just the three of them; but as long as they were together, Maggie could be happy.

Ellen knocked on the door five minutes early. As she introduced herself to Scott and shook his hand, Maggie continued to be impressed by the teen's maturity and began to relax at the thought of leaving her baby in the care of someone else. They gave Ellen a list of instructions and phone numbers and decided to limit their stay at the party to a couple of hours since this was their first time leaving Abby. The couple gave their daughter hugs and kisses before walking out the door. Scott took Maggie's hand as they walked down the front steps to their car.

When the couple pulled up to the department chair's stone house, the party had already begun, and most of the guests were outside enjoying themselves on the side terrace. It was a bit chilly, but a few strategically placed heaters made the outdoors comfortable and inviting. Scott beamed having his wife next to his side. No more making excuses and trying to hide their problems from his colleagues. All those difficult months were behind them, Scott thought, looking to the days ahead.

The first half hour of the party Scott and Maggie spent talking with the other professors at the college. His colleagues and their spouses welcomed Maggie into the college family with their words of support for her as they said, "This must have been a difficult move." Maggie's receptive reaction to the conversation topic surprised Scott and also began to lighten the burden he had taken on, secretly blaming himself for his wife's unhappiness. As the couple moved through the party toward the kitchen, Scott spied Bridget.

Scott never thought to tell Maggie that a month earlier the college had hired a research assistant for him. It wasn't a big deal to Scott, but Bridget was twenty-two, gorgeous, and what Scott didn't know is that she had her eyes set on her new boss, not caring in the least that he already had a family. His heart, though, was with Maggie and Abby, but his lack of disclosure about his new assistant created a new wedge in the couple as well as re-opening the recent wounds of their move. An evening that was supposed to be the couple's re-entrance into happily married life was the beginning of new tensions and resentment.

"Oh, Maggie. There's my assistant. I'd like you to meet her."

"Your assistant?" Maggie said lowering the tone of her voice.

It was a tone Scott had heard only a few times during their marriage and not one of those incidents ended up being a good time. Scott's heart sank thinking this was not going to end well for him, but he did his best to hide his concern.

"You never told me you had an assistant. When did this happen?"

Before Scott could answer, Bridget saw her boss, her face lighting up with a huge smile.

"Scott," she said as she walked toward him, never taking her eyes off him.

Scott made the introduction. "Bridget, this is my wife, Maggie."

"It is so nice to finally meet you. You are all I have heard about this past month."

The smile she gave to Bridget looked sincere on the outside but was full of venom on the inside. Maggie masked her anger with a light-hearted response. "You've had to hear about me for a whole month," she said looking at Scott.

Scott's heart sank again. He had just gotten his wife back and now he felt as though he had lost her again.

Bridget responded full of excitement. "This has been the best month of my life. I feel so fortunate to be able to work with someone as talented as Scott. I've learned so much in such a short time."

Maggie didn't know who she wanted to choke more, her husband or his new assistant.

Still smiling, Maggie said, "That's wonderful that this has been the best month of your life."

"Oh, I'm sorry. I'm being so insensitive talking about how great things have been for me when you've been having such a hard time adjusting. You just take your time and don't worry about a thing. The college has a top-notch cafeteria where Scott can get his meals since you don't cook for him the way you used to."

All of a sudden Scott felt exposed. What seemed like an innocent conversation a few weeks ago now felt like an accusation against Maggie. "Excuse us. There are a lot more people I want to introduce to my wife."

Although Maggie was grateful for Scott ending the conversation, she still couldn't help but feel betrayed by her husband. How dare he reveal intimate details of their marriage to someone he hardly knew, let alone his trampy new assistant? Maggie wished away the rest of the night. She smiled and was pleasant to everyone, seemed to any observer to be having a great time, but inside she was a mess. The hurt Maggie felt made her feel sick to her stomach. The pain in her chest made it difficult for her to even breathe.

When the two hours were up, Maggie and Scott thanked the host and said their goodbyes. Once they got in the car, Scott said, "Maggie, let me explain."

"Oh, you want to explain now after a month has gone by? So now suddenly you want to talk about this? There is nothing you can say."

"Maggie, she is no big deal to me. She might as well be a man. I love you and Abby and the only other important aspect of my life right now is my research, but certainly not my research assistant."

"How can you even say that after you've been sharing such private details of our marriage? How dare you, Scott! Everything you do is hurtful. You move me across the country away from all our friends and family, and then you leave Abby and me in a place we don't even know to spend time with your trampy assistant. I'm done with you. I hate everything about you, Scott."

"Maggie, I understand you're upset."

"No, no you don't understand, Scott, or you wouldn't even have said that. I have really been trying to get our marriage back to the way it was. I thought tonight would be the start of our new life and instead of a fresh beginning, you've ruined everything for us."

They drove the rest of the way in silence. Scott knew he had messed up and deeply regretted not mentioning his assistant to Maggie. Over the past few months he did everything he could to win his wife back and now this. It was the first time Scott ever feared what the future held for his marriage.

CHAPTER 14

Angry people are not always wise.

—Jane Austen

Early the next morning, Maggie headed out for a walk with Abby. She pushed the stroller around the block twice before Jean came out of her house and called to her.

"You're out early this morning."

Maggie was relieved she would finally have someone to talk to about last night. She didn't want to call her family and share the story of the previous evening. She knew they would worry and none of them needed that stress in their life.

She stood on the front porch, "I just came to say good-bye. Abby and I are going back to Montana tomorrow."

"What?"

Maggie burst into tears and sobbed. "I hate my husband. Abby and I need to go back home."

"Oh, dear. Come here."

Jean wrapped her arms around Maggie and let her cry on her shoulder. Once Maggie calmed her sobbing, Jean said "Now let's go inside and talk about this. We can work this out."

Sitting in the living room, she explained the whole evening. "Jean, I'm so hurt. I can't believe Scott did this to me."

"I can see you're hurt, Maggie. I would be hurt, too. It was really bad judgment on his part."

"Yes, it was. Why do men do things like that?"

"Sometimes they're not too bright."

"What do I do?"

"Well, you don't go back to Montana, that's for sure. You stay put."

"How do I stay here when I know Scott is spending eight hours a day with that girl? You should have seen her. She didn't take her eyes off him the entire night. I watched her. She looked like a high school girl trying to get the popular guy to notice her. She doesn't care that Scott's married. That's the thing. Besides not telling me about her, she has her sights on him. How can he not realize that?"

"First, Scott loves you. You even said that she was *trying* to get Scott to notice her. Second, men can be oblivious. You can't run away at the first sign of trouble. Nothing will irritate little Miss Assistant more than knowing each night Scott goes home to you. She would love nothing more than to know you are back in Montana and she has free access to your husband."

"I hear what you're saying, I just don't know how I'm going to forgive Scott for this."

CHAPTER 15

When you know better you do better.

—Maya Angelou

The next morning Jean decided to drink her coffee on her porch and wait for Scott to walk to his car. When he saw Jean, he waved.

"Hi, Scott. How are you?"

Scott was sure Maggie had told Jean about what happened at the party so he was fairly sure he wouldn't get much sympathy, but he needed someone to talk to. "I've been better."

"You and Maggie have been better. Come here. Sit down." Jean motioned to the chair next to her.

"Jean, I don't know what to do. Maggie and I had such a great relationship before this move. We used to do everything together. We went for walks together. We went to the movies. We talked all the time, and now all that has changed." Scott thought he would find Jean difficult to talk to. She was after all Maggie's friend, but instead of condemnation, Scott found acceptance and understanding. He also found in Jean someone he could talk to. Scott continued letting everything that was bottled up inside of him out.

"When Maggie and I first met, I knew right then and there I would marry her. She was, is so beautiful. My friends and I decided to take a trail tour at Glacier. We had lived our entire lives in Montana and had never taken a tour so on this particular day we decided on an adventure. As soon as I got out of my Jeep and saw Maggie round the corner, I think my heart stopped. I was so nervous all of a sudden. I started sweating and my hands were all clammy. I was afraid I'd make a fool of myself. I wanted so badly to talk to her, but I didn't know what to say. I kept looking back at her hoping something clever would come to me, but it didn't, so I kept my mouth shut."

Scott looked like he wanted to continue, but said, "I'm sorry Jean. I'm taking up all of your time."

"Scott, all I have is time. Continue." Jean was enjoying hearing Scott's part of the story, and it gave Jean a good sense about what kind of man he truly was. Jean also knew when a man finally wanted to talk, you let him talk.

"Well, as soon as we got into the Jeep, my friend Derek starts talking about Maggie and how hot she was. Derek was fine as a friend, but I certainly wouldn't trust him around a woman. When we got back to my house, Derek says that he's going to go back to Glacier in the morning and ask Maggie out. I said, 'No, you're not. I'm going to ask her out.' Derek can be a real antagonist and he says, 'Who's going to stop me?' By this time Derek and I are standing across from each other and our other two friends are standing off to the side. So I say, 'I'm going to stop you.' So Derek laughs and takes both hands and pushes me."

"He pushed you? What did you do?"

"I punched him in the face."

Jean started to laugh. "You punched him in the face?" she repeated.

"I don't know what came over me. I guess maybe it was how sweet Maggie was and how I couldn't even think about him putting his hands on her. It drove me nuts. I made sure I got up extra early the next morning so I could be the first one at Glacier just in case Derek's fat lip didn't get the message across and he tried to hit on Maggie."

"So you are a real-life cowboy?"

"How so?"

"You kind of fought a duel over Maggie."

Scott started to laugh. "I guess I did, and I won." He smiled.

"Yes, you did. But Maggie won, too. You're a good man, Scott."

"Thanks, Jean, but Maggie's really upset with me."

"She has a right to be. Maggie's had a tough time lately trying to make life work here for all of you. She gave up a lot for you, Scott. You should have told her about this attractive younger assistant."

"I didn't notice she was attractive."

"I'm eighty-eight years old, Scott. You can't fool me. Men always notice when a woman is attractive."

"What am I going to do? I love Maggie. I'm afraid she's going to leave me."

"Does she have a reason to leave you?"

"My goodness, no. I would never cheat on my wife. I realize I should have told Maggie about the assistant and I should not have opened up about the struggles we were having. That was so stupid. I realize that now. I just don't know what to do."

"Well, you fought for your wife before. You need to do that again."

"How?"

"Scott."

"Yes?"

"Ditch the assistant."

Maggie waited to get out of bed until Scott left for work. She hadn't slept in for months, but Abby woke up late in the morning giving her the extra rest she needed. She looked around her house and thought it needed a fresh cleaning. After she fed the baby, Maggie ran the vacuum, dusted, and straightened up. She spent some time carrying Abby through the house, showing her the décor she chose when they first moved in. Although she knew Abby had no idea what she was saying, it felt good to have her daughter smile as she pointed to pictures and explained her color choices. She had made the house warm, comfortable, and inviting. So far Ellen had been their only guest, and her compliments regarding the home she created meant the world to Maggie. As she walked to the family room, the doorbell rang. She said to Abby, "I wonder who's here."

Maggie looked out the window and seeing Jean standing on the front porch leaning on her cane, she rushed to get the door. Concerned that Jean had walked up the steps alone, she helped Jean into the house.

Out of breath Jean said, "I'm not sure how I made it that whole way."

"Here. Sit down. I'll get you some water and put on a pot of coffee."

"After I get a few minutes of rest, I would love to see what you've done with the house. The living room is lovely, dear."

Maggie handed a glass of water to Jean who took a few sips before handing it back. "That was refreshing, dear. Thank you."

"Can I get you anything else? I can make us some breakfast."

"No thank you. I'm not very hungry."

"Rye toast maybe?"

"Now that sounds good."

"I have some homemade huckleberry jam that my mom sent me. Would you like to try it?"

"I would love to. Thank you."

Maggie moved the bouncy seat to the living room so that Abby and Jean could spend some time together. She poured a cup of coffee for Jean, noticing how the mugs she used were so clunky compared to Jean's delicate teacup set. She put butter and jam on the toast and took the light snack out to her friend.

"I've never had huckleberry jam. This is a treat." Jean took a bite. "This is delicious, Maggie. Please give your mom my compliments."

Maggie sat down on a chair across from Jean thinking she could now relax for a bit, but Abby began to cry. She lifted her baby girl out of her seat, but she kept crying. "Jean,

I'm sorry. I think Abby needs to be changed. I'll be right back."

"Take your time sweetheart, and no need to apologize."

Jean watched as Maggie walked upstairs with the baby and while she was alone she looked around the living room reliving some of the memories of this house and the years past. In her own home Jean felt the absence of her husband and the life she once had, but she was used to it. Here in Maggie's home an unexpected twinge of grief began to work on Jean's heart. She never felt much like crying, but now sitting in Maggie's living room, she was overcome by a sense of loss. The loss of Marty, of the way the neighborhood used to be all hit Jean at once, but she was a strong woman. If she needed to, she could have a cry later. This morning was all about Maggie and what she was facing in her life. That's why Jean worked her way up all those steps in the front of the house. She wasn't going to let old memories spoil this time with her new friend.

Maggie came back downstairs holding Abby in her right arm and holding the railing with her left hand. "You must read minds, Jean. Right before you rang the doorbell, I was walking around the house with Abby thinking that besides Ellen, we haven't had anyone over and now here you are."

"It's been a long time since I've been in this house. It brings back so many happy memories, especially this front room. The grand piano sat in the corner over there," she said pointing behind Maggie.

She turned to look in the corner. "That is a good spot for a piano. Who played it?"

"Eddie and Mike could play. They would take turns while the rest of us sang."

"That sounds like fun. I wish times were still like that."

"It was a unique time and I'm glad I got to experience it. Life is so much harder now. I can't imagine how things will be when Abby is your age. I just pray that the world gets better and people wake up to what is really important in life and just stop all this nonsense."

"You've seen so much change in the world. It's fascinating. Could you ever imagine any of it?"

"Never. The technology, for starters. That was a thing of the movies. It wasn't real life, and now it is. But, that's the catch. Technology is part of real life but it isn't real life. This texting and tweeting. It's not real connection. You know what real connection is, Maggie? This. Sitting face to face, sharing coffee and talking. I came over today because I wanted to see how you were doing. So how are you, Maggie?"

"Okay. I'm feeling a little numb, like the events at the party never happened."

"Have you and Scott talked everything out?"

Maggie laughed. "Hardly. We've barely spoken since the other night."

"Elizabeth and Eddie went through those stages, but they had wonderful times here, as well."

Thinking back to Jean's story, Maggie's curiosity was piqued. "You said something about Elizabeth and Angie. There were problems there?"

"The problem was with Elizabeth. Angie was a good, loyal friend. She didn't want anything to do with Eddie or anyone else's husband for that matter. Things got better once Angie met Frank."

"That's right. I was trying to guess where they met and when I said 'the circus' you said 'close.' I have no idea. I give up."

"Okay. I'll tell you."

CHAPTER 16

If an offense come out of the truth,
better is it that the offense come
than the truth be concealed.

−*Thomas Hardy*

Angie's irritation began to show on her face. She had had enough of Elizabeth's snide remarks, and this evening she just wasn't in the mood. Too bad the parties always seemed to be at Elizabeth's house. Angie wouldn't even be sitting in the Getz's living room if it weren't for all her other friends whom she loved dearly. On this particular evening Elizabeth took everyone's drink order, except for Angie's. She carried the tray of drinks gently stooping down so her guests could remove their glass and as the tray emptied of the last drink, Elizabeth said, "Oh, Angie. I'm so sorry. What would you like?"

Coming from anyone else, this was an innocent oversight, but coming from Elizabeth who was sure every unmarried woman was after her husband, this was a blatant act to make Angie feel uncomfortable. None of Elizabeth's antics ever worked on Angie, though. After witnessing the horrors of the war and holding her best friend during her final moments of life, there was no making Angie feel uncomfortable. Elizabeth didn't realize how silly and insignificant she made herself during these exchanges. Here was a grown woman exposing her insecurity before all of their friends. Angie usually felt sorry for Elizabeth, but tonight she was irritated.

Angie stood up. "Elizabeth, let me be clear with you in front of all of our friends. I have no interest in your husband. I have no interest in anyone else's husband for that matter. Your behavior at the least is unbecoming and for as long as our gatherings are held here in this den of jealousy and insecurity, you can all count me out. Good evening."

Silence fell over the group as they looked from one to another, all eyes finally resting on Elizabeth. Caroline reached for Angie as she walked through the living room and followed her friend to the front door. "Please don't go."

Angie turned and hugged her. "You're a sweetheart, Caroline. I just need to be away from here right now." When she let herself out of the house, the crisp September air refreshed her. It was a Saturday night and the Apple Dumpling Festival had begun, the first night of a week of fun and food.

Back inside the house, Eddie broke his silence. "Do you want to know something Elizabeth? I've had enough of this attitude. Angie is *our* friend and a guest in *our* home and you treat her in such a manner that she leaves? Go apologize to her."

"I am not apologizing to anybody. Besides I have nothing to apologize for."

Jean spoke up. "Yes, you do. Eddie's right. Angie is our friend and we care about her. This isn't what we stand for in our friendship."

Marty stood behind Jean. "I think we've all had enough of this."

"Oh, all right."

Elizabeth went to the front door, called after Angie, and finally caught up to her halfway down the sidewalk.

The entire group stood on the front porch to witness the apology. "Angie, you're right. I've been behaving badly. I'm sorry I treated you that way. You don't deserve it and it wasn't right of me. Please come back inside."

"I accept your apology, Elizabeth. I'll come back some other time. Right now I'm going to head down to the Apple Dumpling Festival."

In a loud voice Elizabeth called up to the group. "We're going to the Apple Dumpling Festival."

Jean and Caroline clasped their hands together in excitement. "We'll grab our sweaters."

The group of friends loved going to the Apple Dumpling Festival. The rides, the games, the food, the favorite of which were the homemade dumplings. They were best served sprinkled with a bit of sugar and a little milk in the bottom of the bowl. The seven friends strolled through the gravel-lined pathways, stopping every so often to play a game. Marty won a giant panda bear for Jean. Mike won three teddy bears for Caroline, and Eddie's baseball skills won nine goldfish for Elizabeth. Jean asked, "Where are you going to put those fish?"

Eddie answered, "I think we still have the bowl we bought last year right around this same time when I won…" Eddie paused for a second and then turned to Elizabeth, "What was it last year? Eight?"

"No, it was seven."

"I think it was eight," Eddie said.

"It was seven. I remember because you named them after the seven dwarves."

"Oh, that's right. Hey, I'm two better this year. Does anyone know where I could find nine names?"

Marty looked at his friend like he had lost his mind. "Are you joking? Aren't there nine players on a baseball team? Didn't you play baseball, Eddie?" he said with a laugh.

"That's right I did." The truth was that he loved his life with Elizabeth and his family and friends. The stability this life gave Eddie got him out of bed every morning. His baseball days were a treasured memory, yet a distant one. Eddie held one of the bags of goldfish up to his face, and pointing at it said, "In honor of my Reading baseball team, for starters, I'm going to call this one Eddie."

Everyone groaned.

Although Angie had planned to come to the festival by herself, she was actually glad for the company of her friends. When they were standing in the cotton candy line, Elizabeth walked to the front next to Angie. "So, a den of jealousy and insecurity?"

She wished that Elizabeth would get her life together and no matter how absurd she behaved, Angie couldn't stay angry at her. "That was a bit harsh of me."

"Actually, it wasn't. I just want to be nice in life and the more I want to be nice, the worse I get."

"For goodness sakes, why, Elizabeth? You have a husband who loves you. You have the most beautiful house in the neighborhood. You have a beautiful wardrobe, an amazing shoe collection, and you're gorgeous. What's there to be mean about?"

"I don't know."

"Is it the letters?"

Elizabeth felt like breaking down right in the cotton candy line. "I think about those letters every day. How dare Suzy!"

"Listen to me. Stop it. Yes, Suzy wrote letters to Eddie, but he only opened one—the one he thought was from you. All those envelopes that you threw on the front lawn—none of them were opened. Stop torturing yourself and stop punishing Eddie for something that a false friend did."

Even after all the uncomfortable behavior that Elizabeth threw at Angie, here she was offering kind, encouraging words. Elizabeth's throat tightened. Angie looked at her and said, "Do not cry. It's okay. Just be happy. Not everyone gets the kind of life you have. Be grateful."

Angie was right. Elizabeth had everything any woman could want. Enough of holding on to all this resentment toward a woman who wasn't even her friend anymore and enough of punishing her husband for something that wasn't his fault. The burden of the years lifted from Elizabeth's shoulders. It was fitting that it was the nurse in the group who healed her of years of wounds.

As the friends approached the carousel, a man came up to them. "Ladies and gentlemen. I oversee the guests we have at the festival, and I'd like to know how you are enjoying yourselves."

As Angie turned to look at the man speaking, the cotton candy fell from her hand onto the ground. Frank felt the connection, too. He rushed to pick up the cotton candy now covered in dirt and cinders. Never had he entertained any other guest at any of his festivals, but there was something about Angie that made him behave in a manner that never crossed his mind before. Frank looked Angie in the eyes, extended his hand, and said, "My dear, I would love to buy you another cotton candy and if you would be so kind as to accompany me, I would love to show you around."

Angie took his outstretched hand and said, "It would be my honor."

The group of friends looked on with mouths hanging open as they walked away. Frank looked back over his should and said, "We'll meet you at the entrance in half an hour."

Half an hour later, they waited as Angie and Frank appeared, with Frank carrying a teddy bear, a giant panda, and three bags filled with goldfish. Angie beamed as Frank said, "I will call you tomorrow." Then to the surprise of everyone, including Angie, Frank kissed her and then said, "and tonight."

Frank stood at the entrance as they walked through the parking lot. Elizabeth walked next to Angie and said, "I apologize if this is too forward, but I think you're in love."

Angie replied with her eyes still shining, "I think you're right.

Frank kept his promise and called Angie that night. They talked for hours and planned to meet the next morning for breakfast. Angie arrived at the Sinking Spring Diner at nine o'clock and seeing Frank already in the parking lot, pulled her car next to his.

He got out of his car and opened Angie's car door for her. She smiled at him, melting his heart. "This has been the best day of my life so far and the day's only just begun."

Arm in arm they walked into the diner together. Over coffee and pancakes they shared details of their war experiences. Frank had been in the Naval Battle for Guadalcanal. Angie listened as Frank described the united effort of the offensive in the Pacific.

Angie's stories of her experiences intrigued Frank. She was the most fascinating woman he had ever met. He knew there was something special about her, but he also knew he would be leaving in a week. The most he could do is treasure the next few days with her.

Frank wanted to show Angie around the festival grounds without all the chaos of the crowds. "Have you ever been to a festival during the off-hours?"

"I can't say that I have."

"I would love to show you around. You can see what the festival is like without the lights, music, and fanfare."

"I'd love to see it."

Angie followed Frank back to the Apple Dumpling Festival. It had a different smell about it. Less food and more fresh air. Angie hadn't noticed the tree cover from the night before, but now in the light of day she was able to enjoy the canopy the trees provided. Children ran up and down the dusty midway in their pajamas and parents called after them to come get breakfast. The festival looked much less magical now, but it still held a pull for Angie. The main pavilion which last night housed picnic tables for the many guests enjoying apple dumplings now held families eating breakfast together. They entered the area with greetings from the workers. Frank got a cup of coffee for Angie and the two of them sat at an empty picnic table.

"So how does all this work?" Angie asked.

"What part? There is a lot that goes into the carnival."

"I wonder how people decide to join a carnival and how do they get paid? There are so many different job responsibilities here."

"To answer your first question, everyone here has a story as to why they are here. See the young thin man sitting at the end of the table right over there?" Frank asked pointing to the far corner of the pavilion.

"Yes."

"That's Danny. His dad used to beat his mother. She refused to leave her husband though, and one day when

Danny came home from high school to his mother sitting at the kitchen table with yet another black eye, he unleashed years of anger, beating his father and sending him to the hospital. He was taken into juvenile custody. Once he got out of the detention center, he tried to convince his mother to leave and find a safe place to live, but she wouldn't go, so Danny left on his own. He wandered from place to place before joining us. He's in charge of all the games. When someone new comes in looking for a job, he's the one who places them. He has a knack for matching people to a job here."

"Is everyone here running from someone or something?"

"No. Not at all. See the family next to us?" Frank said, motioning to a table beside them with a mother, father, and three girls. "The mother and father grew up in the carnival. They were best friends growing up and now they're married and raising their family here. They are trapeze artists."

Angie noticed how happy and content the girls looked. "What about school and learning?"

"All of that is up to the family. Most families teach their children their trade, but also provide some home-school instruction, as well."

"What about food, nutrition, doctors? How are people given care and how do they get their meals?"

"Some families buy their own food and cook for their own families. We provide a meal plan, however. Ken is our resident cook. A lot of singles opt for the meal plan. As far as doctors, if anyone gets sick they need to find a physician in whatever town we are in."

"That doesn't seem very convenient."

"It isn't."

"So how do the workers get paid?"

"It varies. Our main attractions like our acrobats, trapeze artists, and dog trainers get a salary. Any of the food stands pay us a fee out of their profits. The guys in charge of the games make a portion of their quota, but if they don't make the quota, they don't get paid."

"That's rough."

"It is but there is the potential to make a lot of money. The best personalities make the most money. Guys who can't get out and mingle with the crowd and draw them in to play their game usually don't last long. It might seem like a romantic notion to be part of a traveling show, but it takes a lot of skill and effort."

"Do you have anyone who's running from the law?"

"We don't allow that, but I'm sure there are some guys who are on the run. They usually don't last long."

The lives of the people fascinated Angie as she looked around from table to table wondering about each person's story. "So what's your story, Frank? Why did you join?"

"I like it here."

"That's it? You like it here. No other reason?"

There was another reason, but Frank didn't want to tell Angie about Julia.

They were next door neighbors all throughout school. From the time they were in first grade they walked to and from school together. They talked about everything that little kids talk about. They were comfortable with each other from the beginning, and as a child Frank probably knew even back then that he wanted to marry Julia. One day when they were in second grade playing at recess, Frank was in the middle of a baseball game with his friends when Julia came running over to him, crying. Frank noticed one of Julia's braids was shorter than the other.

"What happened to your hair?"

"Joe cut it off," she said between sobs.

Frank left his post at first base, running full speed toward the school bully. Joe was still holding part of Julia's braid and laughing until Frank stopped right in front of him and punched him square in the nose. Blood splattered onto the ground and Joe ran away crying with blood dripping onto his shirt. Frank was sent home from school and at the end of the day he watched out the window for Julia. Her eyes were still red from crying and her cheeks stained with tears. Instead of turning into her walkway, she walked a few extra feet up the sidewalk to Frank's walkway. He ran down the steps as fast as he could and opened the door before Julia could even knock.

Standing on the front porch, she said to Frank, "Thank you for punching Joe. Seeing him cry made me feel better." Then Julia threw her arms around his neck and hugged him. Frank watched Julia walk back to her house. She waved to him from her front door before turning to go inside.

Frank wasn't sure what his father would say when he got home. Before they ate dinner, his parents sat him down in the living room. His dad said, "Frank, you know we don't condone fighting in this house, but in this case you were standing up for your friend. Coming to Julia's defense was very admirable and chivalrous of you. Her mother called us to thank you for coming to Julia's rescue. Let's go have dinner."

That night they ate dinner together, and for dessert his mother had made him his favorite chocolate cake. She even cut him a bigger piece than he was usually allowed.

Joe the bully never bothered Julia or Frank again. Actually, he never bothered anyone again. After the class watched him run away crying with blood gushing from his nose, he wasn't so intimidating anymore.

Having his mother and father call him chivalrous made a lasting impression on Frank. It became a way of life to Frank, and anyone who ever met him, male or female, felt a sense of noble character coming from him. Frank carried that noble character with him into the war. Knowing that Julia was back home waiting for him made being away easier. What Frank didn't know is while he was away, Julia and his best friend were growing close; at first spending time together for comfort, and then spending time together because they were falling in love.

From the quiet of the waiting before a battle to the sound of bombs and gunfire exploding around him during battle—he pushed himself on day after day, looking ahead to when he would spend the rest of his life with Julia. The scent of her hair, the feel of her arms around him, the sound of her laugh carried Frank through every battle, every offensive, every attack.

When Frank returned from the war, he stepped off the plane, finally on American ground, and said to himself, *home.* He hailed a taxi and when he got out of the cab in front of his house, he saw Julia and Tommy sitting on her front porch. Frank knew something was wrong when fear spread across their faces instead of joy. Once on the porch Frank noticed the tears in Julia's eyes and the diamond ring on her finger. Frank took Julia by the hand, looked his friend in the eyes and said, "I hope the two of you have a happy life together." He walked down the steps toward his yard while Julia yelled after him, "We didn't mean for this to happen, Frank. It just did. Please don't be mad."

Frank kept walking, never turning around. When he walked into his house, his mother was hosting a tea with some of her friends. She dropped a plate full of cookies and ran to her son. "Frank!" she yelled, and then, crying, hugged him and wouldn't let go. All the other women began crying, and then the questions started. "How are you? Are you hungry? What can we get you?"

He had tears in his eyes, but not from this current homecoming. These tears were because the girl who he had grown up with, the one he had loved and trusted, had broken his heart. This would be the last of his tears for Julia. He took a deep breath, looked at the plate of cookies on the floor and said, "If you have more chocolate chip cookies, I would sure love some." There was a flurry of activity to get the extra batch of cookies from the kitchen and to clean up the mess on the floor.

Sitting in the living room with his mother and her friends, Frank answered every question with patience and grace. He stayed with his parents for a few days and then when the carnival came to town, he made his plans to leave with them. He still kept in touch with his parents, but the traveling carnival meant he was never in one place for long and there would be no more broken hearts in his life. No one would get the chance. He wasn't around long enough, and what woman would actually travel with him in the carnival?

Angie and Frank saw each other every day that the fair was still in town. They were so comfortable with each other that they could share their war stories with one another, stories they had not shared with anyone else. Angie knew all this opening up to Frank was making her vulnerable to the hurt she would feel when he left town, but no matter how much she tried to hold back, she just couldn't. Angie resigned herself to enjoying the short amount of time they were together, but she kept asking why she had to meet the man of her dreams this way? Angie realized there was no way that Frank would stay. What could she possibly say to him? Frank would walk out of her life and where would that leave her? The only answer she had: *alone.*

For the first time since Julia, Frank felt himself falling in love. The days he spent with Angie were fulfilling even if they just walked through the carnival not saying a word. Just being with Angie brought meaning to his life. Frank didn't know how to leave on Sunday. What would he say to Angie? How could he bring himself to say goodbye? Did she feel the same way about him? But he had a plan and all his questions would be answered on Friday evening.

Friday and Saturday were the last nights of the Apple Dumpling Festival. The company had been in town for a week and would be leaving Sunday morning for Harveys Lake near the Poconos, and then the following weekend for upstate New York. Frank picked Angie up at her house to take her out to an early dinner. As they sat talking and avoiding the stress of parting soon, Frank looked back on the years he spent alone, the years he spent trying to forget about Julia. Those were hard years, lonely years. Even though he was always surrounded by people, he was still essentially by himself, isolated emotionally. The more Frank got to know Angie, the more he realized she was unlike any other woman he had ever met. She had a depth to her soul and a grace about her that intrigued him. She had a mystery and an openness about her at the same time. By the end of the week, Julia was a distant memory and he would never dwell on losing her again.

On the drive to the grounds of the Apple Dumpling Festival Frank said, "Tonight is exactly a week since we met. It's been the best week of my life."

"Mine, too."

They drove the rest of the way in silence and when they arrived at the carnival, sounds of rides and laughter greeted them.

"I never get tired of that, hearing the happiness that comes from a fair. All of the families and friends together," he said smiling.

The two wound their way down the gravel paths enjoying each other's company. Near the end of the evening, he turned to Angie and took her by the hands. "I've been doing some thinking."

"Oh, really? About?"

"About us. Angie I was wondering…"

"Yes."

"What do you mean, 'yes'? You don't even know what I'm going to ask you. What if it's something horrible?"

"I know it isn't, so the answer is yes."

"Can I at least ask you my question first?"

"Yes."

Frank smiled. "Angie, I would be honored if you would join our company as our nurse."

Not exactly the question she was hoping for, but it did seem promising. Angie smiled. "Frank, that's brilliant. I have been trying to come up with a way that we didn't have to part, but it seemed hopeless. Now, here you are with the answer. I would love to join your company."

"I have another question for you."

Her heart skipped and she tried to remain composed. "If it's as good as the first question, the answer is yes again."

"Angie, will you marry me?"

CHAPTER 17

Friendship is a sheltering tree.
—Samuel Taylor Coleridge

W ell, what did Angie say?"
Jean laughed. "She said yes, of course, and right after she said yes, the evening's fireworks show began, so it was all very cliché and romantic."

"And perfect."

"And perfect. Angie deserved perfect."

"Then what happened? How did all of this go? That was a huge step to leave everything she knew and just pick up and leave." Maggie thought for a moment about her own steps, leaving everything and everyone she knew.

"Angie called me that night to tell me the good news and to ask me to help her pack. We threw a party for the happy couple on Saturday night and then on Sunday morning, they headed out on their next adventure."

"Did you ever see them again?"

"Oh yes. Angie kept her house. We looked after it while she was gone, and periodically Frank and Angie would stay for a week or two between bookings. It was a blessing that we were able to spend time with the two of them. They were very happy together and Angie found where she belonged. During the war Angie was used to moving from place to place and setting up camp and triage in some rather brutal environments. For her experiencing the excitement of traveling and new places in peacetime while practicing nursing— well, it was the perfect fit. I think we all have a place where we fit in during our lives, and everything we've experienced up to that time has prepared us for where we are truly meant to be. Angie's life shows that."

"Hmmm. Interesting. That was a nice story, Jean. Thanks for cheering me up."

"Anytime, dear. Now, I'm getting a little tired."

Maggie took Abby up to her crib for a nap. As soon as Abby's head touched the mattress, she was asleep. Maggie went back downstairs to help Jean to her house.

"How is our little angel?"

Maggie liked how Jean called Abby *our* little angel. It felt like she was part of their family, and being so far away from hers, it was a comfort to Jean as well. "She's fast asleep."

"I hope I didn't bore her."

Maggie laughed. "No way. Abby adores you. And both of us love your stories. Speaking of which, you have one more to tell."

"Only one more? It went so fast."

"It did, and I still want to hear that last story."

"Ah, yes. Mike and Caroline."

As Maggie helped Jean maneuver the steps on her front walkway, she asked, "Where did they live again?"

Jean pointed a few doors up the street to a stone house. "Right up there, dear."

"Who lives there now?"

"A single, very good-looking man by the name of David. I used to sit on my porch and watch him go to work. It was the best part of my day."

"Jean!" Maggie laughed.

"If you didn't have that handsome husband of your own, I'd say it might be the best part of your day, too."

Jean and Maggie were both laughing now.

Maggie wondered how long it had been since Jean was able to get out of her house.

"Have you ever had a Starbucks coffee?"

"No."

"How about I take you tomorrow morning? I think you would enjoy it."

"Gosh, most of my outings have been to the doctor's office these past few months. A coffee shop sounds like a wonderful treat. Thank you."

"I'll pick you up at eight o'clock."

"I'll be waiting."

Jean was sitting on her porch when Maggie pulled her car up to the house. As soon as Jean saw her friend, she grabbed her cane and started up the walkway to the sidewalk. Maggie got out of the car. "Let me help you." She helped the elderly woman get settled in the passenger seat and then checked in the back to see Abby wide awake looking out the window.

"This is fun already and we're not even there yet."

"I think you're really going to like this coffee."

"I'm from the Second World War era. We're particular about our coffee. We'll see."

As always, the Starbucks parking lot was full, but Maggie found a parking space close to the door so Jean wouldn't have to walk far. She seemed to be a little slower today.

"Are you feeling okay?"

"My legs are bothering me a little bit."

"Why don't we go back to the car and just go to the drive-thru."

"I'm fine, dear. It feels nice to be out. I'd like to go in."

Maggie carried Abby in her seat while holding on to Jean with her other arm. A man dressed in a business suit held the door for them. Both women thanked him at the same time. He smiled and closed the door gently behind him.

"We can sit at a table or there are some nice leather chairs over there."

"The leather chairs look very comfortable, but I'm afraid I'll never be able to get up once I'm in. Let's sit at that table over there. There's enough room for Abby's seat, too."

Jean sat down and Maggie put Abby's seat on the chair next to her. "What kind of coffee would you like?"

"Whatever you usually get."

"Coffee with cream."

"Make that two."

"Wow, Jean. Coffee with cream? This will be totally new for you."

"Well, Maggie, I've decided to start living life on the edge. At my age adding cream to coffee after drinking it black for seventy-five years is as edgy as I get."

Maggie carried two Grande cups back to the table. "This is the moment of truth."

Jean brought the cup up to her lips and took a sip. Her eyes lit up and she took another sip. "Oh, that's good coffee."

Maggie smiled. "I thought you would like Starbucks coffee."

"Like it, I love it. This coffee has some guts to it."

Jean seemed to perk up after a few minutes. Maggie asked, "How are you feeling today?"

"Better now. I was a little tired this morning, but being out feels very good. I like it here."

"I'm glad. See, the younger generation knows how to connect."

"Maggie, look around. We're the only two here without a phone or computer."

"Oh, boy. You're right."

Jean held up her coffee cup for a toast. "Here's to us, baby."

"To us, Jean."

They sat enjoying their coffee for a few more minutes. "How are things between you and Scott?"

"They are getting better, but not great. I do have good news, though. Scott had his research assistant transferred."

"That's great news. How did he manage that?" Jean asked raising her eyebrows.

"An email went through to the Science Department that several graduate students needed placement. Scott agreed to take two first-year male students under his direction and suggested a move for his research assistant. So now she is in another wing of the building and their paths never cross."

"Attaboy, Scott. I like that man's style. So why are things not great if little what's-her-name is out of the picture?"

"I don't know, Jean. I just get so down sometimes and I guess I blame Scott."

"You shouldn't do that, Maggie. Life is too short to be down in the dumps. I've lived a long time, and looking back, even through hard times I still say that life is too short to spend it upset. Start building your relationship back up. One day when you look back on your life you will see that Scott is all you have. Kids leave and start families of their own and live their own lives."

Maggie knew Jean was right. Why couldn't she build up the courage to just forgive her husband and move on in their marriage?

Maggie drove back to their neighborhood and with Abby in her arms helped Jean to her front door. "Do you need some help once you're inside? I can make lunch for you if you're hungry."

"The coffee filled me up, so I'm not very hungry. I'll probably just rest for a while. I had a lovely morning, Maggie. Thank you so much for taking me out for coffee. It was just so nice to spend this time with you and Abby. She is such a treasure."

"It was my pleasure. I hope we can go out again soon."

Maggie guided Jean to the sofa and helped her sit down. "Are you sure I can't get you anything?"

"No. I'm good right here."

Maggie hated to leave. She felt an overwhelming sense of dread, but she couldn't identify where it was coming from.

"Maggie, what's bothering you?"

"I don't know. I feel so bad about leaving you here alone."

"I'm fine. Really. I'm simply tired. My nights are a little rough sometimes. I just need a little rest. Knowing you're enjoying your day with your daughter will make me feel better."

Although she was reluctant to leave, Maggie headed toward the door. "Call me if you need anything. I'll check on you later."

When Scott returned home after a day of work, it was getting dark and his wife was standing on the front porch. He got out of his car and asked, "Is everything okay, Maggie?"

"I don't know. I'm worried about Jean. She seemed extra tired today and I just have this awful feeling in my stomach that I can't get rid of."

"Did you call her?"

"No." Back inside, Maggie picked up her cellphone to call Jean. The phone rang and rang on the other end with no answer. Maggie hung up and paced across the living room keeping her eyes on Jean's house.

Scott sensed his wife's concern. "Why don't I go down to Jean's house and check on her?"

"I'll get Abby. We can check on her together." Maggie wasn't sure what she would find at Jean's house, but she didn't want to be alone. Scott held their daughter while Maggie looked in the dining room window.

"Do you see anything?"

"No, it's too dark. I don't want to scare Jean. Can you imagine her seeing someone looking in the window?"

They stood on the front porch for a minute. Scott said, "Doesn't Jean have one of those call devices if she's in trouble?"

"Yes. She always keeps it on her when she's in the house."

"Well, if she were in trouble, 911 would be notified. She's probably just sleeping. You said she was extra tired today."

"She was, but I don't know, Scott. I just feel like something's wrong."

Scott knew that nothing he said would reassure Maggie that Jean was fine, and he was beginning to get worried himself. The house was dark, too dark. "Here, hold Abby. I'm going back to the house for a flashlight."

While Scott ran back to their house, Maggie peeked through windows trying to see into the living room. Jean always had lights on and she usually kept the living room light on all night, but there wasn't a hint of light coming from anywhere.

Scott returned with the heavy-duty flashlight he kept in their bedroom in case of a power outage. He shined it through the window on the top half of the front door. The living room was empty.

Maggie said, "I can't see anything. Can you?"

"No. Could Jean have gone out somewhere?"

"I think she would have mentioned that to me at some point during our time together today."

"Maybe she's sleeping."

Maggie still had an uneasy feeling. "Let's just look one more time."

Scott shined the light into the living room once more, methodically scanning the room and the part of the hallway leading back to Jean's room. "I still don't see anything. Do you?"

"No. Let's look in the dining room before we leave."

Half joking Scott said, "Or before someone calls the cops."

They carefully scanned the dining room. The table and chairs were neatly pushed in as always. Nothing seemed out of the ordinary.

"Can you shine the light into the kitchen?" Maggie asked Scott.

As the flashlight lit up part of the kitchen, a slight movement caught Maggie's eye. "Scott, did you see that? Shine the light on the floor right there," Maggie said pointing to the small space in between the dining room and kitchen. As the light rested on the floor, Maggie's knees went weak, "Scott, it's Jean. She's on the floor." Maggie took her phone from her pocket and called 911.

Scott tried the front door, but it was locked. "Stand over there. I'm going to break the window." Maggie walked into the yard and turned her back to the door, shielding Abby. Scott took the flashlight and broke one of the panes of glass. He reached in to unlock the door. Once they made their way inside the house, they heard Jean moaning. Maggie turned on the kitchen light and knelt next to her friend, taking her hand. Maggie gave the 911 operator as many details as she could.

"Oh, Maggie. Thank goodness you're here. I think I broke my hip."

Scott took Abby out of Maggie's arms so she could comfort her friend. "An ambulance is on its way. Just stay still. Don't move."

"Don't worry. I can't move. I've been here all afternoon."

"Jean, I am so sorry. I feel so bad about this."

"Honey, it's not your fault. I'm the one who's old and can't walk."

Even in this state with a broken hip and incredible pain, Jean still cracked jokes.

"You're going to be okay. We'll get you fixed up in no time."

The EMT crew arrived and stabilized Jean. As they carried her to the ambulance on a stretcher, they reassured her. Scott said, "We'll get your window fixed. I don't want you to worry about a thing."

Jean struggled to talk through her pain. "I'm not worried about that Scott. I'm just glad you and Maggie didn't give up. I could hear you talking on the porch and I was so hoping and praying you would find me. I was in too much pain to call out."

"Maggie knew something was wrong. There was no way she was going to leave."

"That's a good woman you have there."

Scott turned to Maggie. "Why don't you go with Jean. Call me, and I'll pick you up from the hospital."

"Okay. Thank you."

The EMTs put Jean in the back of the ambulance and Scott helped Maggie climb in. He stood and watched the ambulance as it pulled away. He felt sick about Jean lying on the floor for hours in all that pain and suffering. What if they had given up? She would have been there all night. Scott pushed that thought out of his mind. They were able to get Jean the help she needed and that's what counted.

During the ambulance ride to the hospital, Jean asked Maggie to call her son in Florida.

"Bobby's number is in my purse. Can you call him and let him know what's going on?"

"Sure, Jean. I'll call once we get to the hospital."

While Jean was taken for x-rays, Maggie waited in the hallway. They had such a fun morning together, but the day took an ugly turn and if she and Scott hadn't checked in on Jean…Maggie stopped in the middle of that thought. A few minutes later a nurse steered the gurney into the hall and Maggie followed them to a room.

The nurse said, "As soon as the doctor looks over the film, he'll be in to talk with you."

She turned to Maggie, "Can I get you anything? A soda or some tea maybe?"

"Thank you, but I'm fine."

The nurse left and Maggie asked, "Are you in pain?"

"Yes, I'm in pain. I feel very uncomfortable."

"I feel so bad about this."

"Aw, honey. This is what happens when people get older. It's no fun. I'm just so grateful you found me. Thank you for not giving up."

The doctor walked into the room stopping the conversation. He put his hand on Jean's shoulder and said, "Well, my dear, it looks like your hip is broken and you're going to need surgery."

"I thought so."

"I'm going to have a nurse give you some medicine to relax you, and then in an hour we'll start the surgery and get you all fixed and back to normal."

Jean said, "Well, I don't know about getting me back to normal. That would take more than hip surgery."

"You have a good sense of humor. I like that. I'll be seeing you soon." With that the doctor left.

"Maggie, can you dial Bobby's number so I can tell him what's going on?"

She handed Jean her cellphone and stood in the hallway to give her some privacy.

Maggie thought about the long road her friend had ahead of her. She would help Jean get through this any way she could. After a few minutes Jean called to Maggie. She went back into the room. "Bobby is going to call the rest of the family. He's going to try to get here tomorrow."

The nurse appeared a minute later. "Hi. I'm Courtney. I'm going to take you to surgery now."

"Can I go along?"

"You can go as far as the hallway leading up to the operating room."

Maggie walked beside Jean. She felt worried and scared, but she tried not to let it show. Once they were in the elevator, Jean took her hand. "Don't worry about me dear. I'm going to be fine. I'm in good hands here."

All of this happened so fast, Maggie was having a difficult time staying strong for her friend. Jean was the one with the broken hip and here she was comforting Maggie. She continued to hold Jean's hand even after the elevator opened. As the nurse pushed the bed down the hall toward double doors, she said, "The operating room is just ahead."

Maggie had been preparing herself for what she would say to Jean when they parted. She tried not to cry but as soon as she started to talk the tears rolled down her cheeks. Once again Jean proved to be the stronger one. "Honey, don't cry. I told you I'm going to be fine."

"I just feel so bad this happened to you."

"It isn't pleasant, but at least I had my make-up on." Jean turned to the nurse, "You should have seen how cute the EMT guys were. I looked up and I thought 'Boy, oh, boy. All these good-looking guys here to rescue me.'"

Maggie and Courtney burst into laughter. Courtney said, "If you think the EMTs were cute, wait until you see the surgeon."

"Then what are we waiting for?" Jean turned to her friend. "See, Maggie. I'm in good hands. Now you go get some rest and I will see you soon."

"I love you, Jean."

"I love you too, dear."

Courtney turned to Maggie. "We'll take good care of her."

Maggie watched as the nurse wheeled the gurney through the double doors and when the doors closed, she walked back to the elevator. Her throat tightened as she tried not to cry. She pressed the button for the first floor and made her way to the gift shop. She wanted Jean to have something nice when she got out of surgery. A bright yellow smiley face mug filled with daisies caught her attention. The bulky mug could never compare to Jean's delicate teacups, but she hoped the mug would welcome her out of surgery. The woman at the gift shop assured Maggie that the flowers would be ready and waiting. She called her husband and he picked her up in front of the hospital. Abby was asleep in her car seat. Scott asked, "How's Jean?"

"She was amazing of course. Cracking jokes and more concerned about how I was doing than her own pain."

"Jean is one tough lady. She'll be fine. Let's get you some dinner and some rest and then tomorrow morning you can check in on her first thing."

As Scott they pulled away from the hospital, Maggie said a silent prayer for her friend.

CHAPTER 18

Old age is like climbing a mountain. You climb from ledge to ledge.
The higher you get, the more tired and breathless you become,
but your views become more extensive.

−Ingmar Bergman

Maggie went to the hospital as soon as visiting hours began. As she got closer to Jean's room, she heard talking and laughing and quietly walked past the door. Jean was propped up in bed, eyes open and a smile on her face, with her family surrounding her. Maggie continued down the hallway and stopped at the nurses' station. "Hi. I'm Jean's friend and neighbor."

One of the nurses responded. "Are you Maggie?"

"Yes."

"Jean told us that when you came in she wanted to see you."

"Oh. Well, her family is in with her now. I thought maybe I could come back later."

"Jean was hoping you would come in while her family was here. She wants them to meet you. Come with me. I'll walk you down."

The nurse leaned into the room. "You have another visitor."

Jean lifted her head. "Maggie. Everyone, this is Maggie."

Introductions went around as Jean's sons, daughters-in-law, and granddaughters welcomed her and thanked Maggie for all her help these past few months.

She stood beside Jean. "How are you feeling?"

"Better than yesterday, that's for sure."

Bobby gave the prognosis. "The doctor said that Mom will be here for a week and then she will be transferred to a rehabilitation center for another week. We are trying to talk Mom into moving to Florida to live with us."

Jean chimed in. "I told you I'm not going anywhere. This is where I grew up and where all my memories are."

Bobby didn't want to upset his mother. "Okay, Mom, but our offer stands as it always has. We love you and we want you to be happy."

"I'm happy here and I don't want anyone worrying about me. Besides, I have Maggie to help me."

"I'll help in any way I can." Maggie turned to Jean's family. She wanted to give them some time alone. "It was nice meeting all of you. I need to get back home."

"Thank you for coming to see me, dear."

Jean's sons walked Maggie into the hallway. Bobby said, "We can't thank you enough for helping our mother. If you hadn't been there, we would have been getting a much different call."

"I'm just glad Jean's getting the help and support she needs. Your mother talks about all of you all the time."

"Our mother speaks very highly of you. She really values your friendship."

"The feeling is mutual. We've had some good times together."

"We'll be here for a few more days and then we'll be heading back to Florida."

"Don't worry. I'll check in on your mom."

Over the next week, Maggie visited Jean in the hospital, and on one special occasion, took her a Starbucks Grande coffee with cream. "You spoil me, Maggie."

"You deserve to be spoiled." The room was empty except for the two women. "Where is everyone?"

"They went out for a nice dinner. They'll be back soon to say goodbye. They're heading home tomorrow."

"I'm sorry to hear that."

"They have work and the kids have school. It was nice getting to see them again. Having everyone together was a blessing to me."

"How are you feeling?"

"To be honest Maggie, I'm tired. I'm really going to try to get some rest after my family leaves."

"I'll let you get some rest, too. Why don't you call me if you need anything. I'll visit the day after tomorrow. That way you get a full day of rest."

"That would be good, dear. It's a date."

Maggie kissed Jean on the forehead. "I'll see you in a couple of days. Please tell your family that I enjoyed meeting them."

"I will, dear."

Maggie spent the next two days taking Abby for walks in her stroller. The weather was still damp, but spring was looming in the air. Abby was wrapped in a blanket and asleep in the stroller. Maggie remembered the first time she took this route when they moved here. It was when she met Jean. Although they had only been in Pennsylvania a few short months, with the stories that Jean shared about her and her friends, it seemed as though she had lived here for years. Maggie looked forward to the next day when she would visit Jean. Even though things still were not great in their marriage, Maggie had to admit that her husband had been supportive through this whole ordeal with Jean, and she was right. Maggie had to work her way back to a good relationship with her husband.

She thought back to their first date. Scott picked her up in his red Jeep and they drove with the top down winding their way to one of the lodges in Glacier National Park. He reserved a table for them on the porch overlooking a lake. Maggie remembered the comfortable feeling both of them had during the drive to the restaurant and during the course of dinner. They talked about their summer jobs and their plans for the future. After dinner they walked down to the lake and sat on the water's edge. It was still light and would be until at least ten o'clock.

"Would you like to go for a drive? I would love to show you where I work."

They walked to the Jeep and drove back roads along a stream. There was a clearing among the trees and small parking area off to the right. Scott pulled into the lot and they got out.

"Well, this is it. The best fly-fishing spot in all of Montana." Scott led Maggie to the stream.

"Proof that pristine beauty still exists." Maggie looked at the water. "So what is the name of the company you work for?"

"Highlander Fly-Fishing Outfitters."

"And how did you get interested in fly-fishing?"

"My dad used to take me fly-fishing when I was a kid. He taught me how to make my own flies and how to tie the knots on the line. I started working at Highlander when I was sixteen, and for a while I thought maybe I would quit school and just work here for the rest of my life."

"Why didn't you?"

"One reason. My dad would have killed me."

Maggie laughed. "I understand. Sometimes when I'm riding a horse through the trails of Glacier I think I could do that forever and I consider not going back to school, but the thought of telling my mom and dad gets rid of any romantic notions I have about being a cowgirl."

"I've seen you at work as a cowgirl. You're quite impressive."

"Well thank you. You make a good cowboy."

Scott acted like he was tipping a hat. "That's mighty kind of you ma'am." Then he added, "I work tomorrow until five; how about I pick you up in my Jeep and we head out of town and find a nice restaurant somewhere?"

Maggie agreed to the date, but she was already thinking about how she would surprise Scott tomorrow at work, just like he surprised her.

The next morning she drove to the Highlander Fly-Fishing Outfitters headquarters. A group had gathered in the lobby for a day of fly-fishing instruction. As Scott approached the group, Maggie stood in the back. Scott introduced himself and showed the eagerly awaiting anglers where they could rent supplies if they didn't have their own. As the group went their separate ways to look at rods, reels, and flies, Maggie made her way to Scott. "Excuse me, I might need some help."

"Maggie!" Without hesitation he hugged her. "This is a nice surprise."

"Thank you. I thought I would see what it's like to be a fly fisherman for a day."

"You've come to the right place. Let's get you set up with our finest rod."

Scott showed Maggie around the store before the group amassed on the bus. They drove to the same location as the previous evening. Scott and another guide each took half of the group, but he made sure Maggie was in his group. Instead of going right to the water's edge, Scott gathered everyone to practice in the grass first.

"Okay, everyone. Spread out and give each other some room." Scott waited while the group lined up far enough away from the person next to them. "First, we'll work on the cast. In fly-fishing you cast the line, not the lure. In wheel fishing the lure has weight, but in fly-fishing the fly has no weight. There is also no wrist in casting. It's all in the fore-arm. Relax your grip on the cork and keep your thumb on top. Remember, where the thumb is pointed, the line goes."

The group practiced in the small clearing before heading to the water. Everyone found a separate space along the water's edge. Scott made his way over to Maggie and standing behind her and holding her right arm with his right hand, he made the casting motion for her. "Just keep repeating this motion a few times and then let the fly come to a rest on the water."

"I love this. Do you think I'll catch anything?"

Scott smiled. "Do I count?"

"If you were on the other end of my line, then yes."

"Okay, well let me make my way downstream."

"You're smooth, Cowboy."

"First time in my life, but better late than never." Always the instructor, Scott gave Maggie a few more pointers. "Cast again a few more times and then let the fly rest on the water again. I'm going to go help some other people, but I'll be back."

Maggie paid more attention to watching Scott than to watching her casting technique, so when a trout took her bait and started pulling on the line, she nearly lost the rod. Scott heard the commotion and quickly ran to her. "Here, like this," he said as he stood behind Maggie, helping her reel in her catch. Maggie felt the strength of Scott's physique behind her, making it difficult to concentrate on the trout. Scott ended up doing most of the work and when he had the trout in front of them, he gently took the fly out of the mouth of the fish.

"You caught a nice trout."

Scott held the fish in the water for a few seconds so Maggie could get a good look. "We let the fish go, so get a good look so you can tell your friends."

"As much as I would love to say I caught that trout, I'm afraid I can't take the credit. You did all the work," she said as she realized she had been so preoccupied with watching Scott that she had no idea there was a trout on her line. Some fisherman.

"You did the hard part Maggie. Not everyone can attract a trout to a fly."

Scott had a sincere smile that said he was a genuine, nice guy. The rest of the day went quickly and before the group knew it, the fishing expedition was over and they were back in Highlander's lobby.

As arranged the night before, Scott picked up Maggie to take her out to dinner. They drove to an A-frame log cabin-style restaurant with a wrap-around deck and a view of the Rocky Mountains. They sat outside at a table on the deck. As on the previous night, Maggie noticed their obvious comfort with one another. Since the sun doesn't set in the Montana summer until ten o'clock, they had plenty of light to enjoy the mountain scenery during dinner and on their way back to Maggie's house. Scott parked his Jeep and walked her to her front door.

They stood facing each other. "This has been the best day of my life."

Maggie smiled. "It was a very, very good day."

Before Maggie could say anything else, Scott took her in his arms and kissed her. With his arms stilled wrapped around her, Scott said, "I just want you to know that one day I'm going to ask you to marry me."

Maggie watched as Scott walked back to his car and drove away. She knew even at the start of their relationship that he was the one—kind and gentle, but strong and tough at the same time. Maggie felt safe with Scott, but not a boring safe. The kind of safe that said they could accomplish anything in this world as long as they were together.

Maggie thought about Jean's life and the woman who had lived and experienced so much. What were the rough spots in her marriage to Marty? Were there any? Had they started out perfect and just continued on that way throughout the rest of their lives? Maggie thought about her own relationship and how when things start out in a perfect way, it's hard when what seemed to be without blemish, now seems to have cracks and dents. Scott had been trying to fill those cracks and dents, but Maggie did her best to undo his work. It was time to take some steps herself and get their marriage back to the comfortable love they once had for each other.

CHAPTER 19

In death a hero, as in life a friend!

−Alexander Pope

W hat do you mean, 'Jean's been moved to ICU'?"
Maggie asked the nurse.

"This happens sometimes with older patients after surgery. Their immune systems are weakened and they become susceptible to pneumonia."

Maggie stood in disbelief. How did this happen to her friend so fast and why wasn't she notified?

She wound her way through the hospital to the ICU, stopping at the nurses' station—thankful that her name was on a list for visitors. To protect the patients from any further contagions, Maggie put on booties over her shoes and a smock over her clothes. She wore a mask to cover her mouth. She hoped Jean would recognize her.

Jean was lying in bed propped up with pillows, her eyes closed. Maggie quietly moved a chair next to the bed and sat silently watching Jean's shallow breathing. After a few minutes she opened her eyes.

"Oh, Maggie. You're here. I've been waiting for you."

"I didn't know. No one told me."

"I know. I've been trying to get better and I knew you would be here today, so I waited."

"You waited?" Fear filled her chest. "Waited for what?"

"I have one more story to tell you."

"Just rest. Get your strength back and then you can tell me the story when you're all better and we're sitting on your porch enjoying coffee and watching your bluebirds."

"Maggie, I have to tell you now. I don't have much longer."

"No. You're fine. Just wait until you get your strength back."

"I'm not going to get my strength back. I've been waiting to tell you this last story. Now, take that mask off your face. You're way too beautiful to be covering it."

Maggie pulled the mask down around her neck.

Jean lifted her hand to Maggie's check. "See, now that's better. Are you ready to hear about Mike and Caroline?"

Maggie took Jean's hand and looked her friend in the eyes, her throat tight and tears running down her face.

CHAPTER 20

Diseases of the soul are more dangerous and more numerous than those of the body.

— Cicero

Mike had always wanted to be in the military. Ever since he was a kid, he dreamed about a life as an Army officer. Mike was diagnosed with hearing loss in both ears as a young child, but he had been able to overcome this challenge, becoming an accomplished pianist and rising to the top of his class in high school. He was confident that the methods he implemented in school in overcoming his hearing loss would translate over into the military. A few months before graduation, he filled out a military application and waited. It didn't take long for a response and in a matter of weeks Mike was at the Military Entrance Processing Station for his physical. The medical exam went well until the hearing test. The test required a response to instructions transmitted via headphones as opposed to face-to-face verbal instructions. Mike tried to respond correctly to the audio, struggling to pass the test, but he just couldn't hear and without someone speaking in front of him, he couldn't even get by on reading lips. The exam turned out to be a disaster and Mike felt his confidence quickly wane. The doctor stopped the exam and said, "You can get dressed." The doctor sat him down in his office and said, "How long have you had difficulty hearing?"

"All my life. I've gotten good at adjusting to it and I'm sure I could overcome this if I'm given a chance in the Army."

"The best I can do is send your medical forms to the Office of the Surgeon General for review and perhaps you might get a chance to serve in the Army, but there are other options, as well. There is industry out there looking for good workers, and you would be an asset to some of these businesses. Your high school transcripts are impressive and you're obviously a very talented and intelligent young man. I would be happy to get some contacts for you."

Mike had a difficult time letting the reality of the situation sink in. He had been preparing for the military all year, keeping in shape and working hard in school. He wasn't ready to accept that he had failed. He tried not to let the disappointment show in his voice, but he had no intention of being passed on to some other industry. Mike feigned interest. "Thanks. That would be helpful."

Mike's dad owned a car dealership. Immediately after graduation he went to work for his father. He made a decent living and saved up a good sum of money while he was living with his parents. His father was proud to have his son working for him and he thought Mike was happy too, but every day that Mike walked into the showroom, he was reminded of his failed dreams. There was one mechanic at the shop, a few years older, who seemed to see through his pain. Mike's dad hired Marty to work at the dealership after seeing him work miracles on a racecar at the local racetrack. During a pit stop Marty led the team with efficiency and the car roared out of the pit in record time; the driver came back to win the race. Mike's dad needed someone like Marty on his team. The pair became instant friends, and it was Marty's sense of humor and easy-going nature that made walking into the dealership each day bearable. He always arrived at work early, and only Mike's dad beat Marty into the dealership. Mike came in a close third and looked forward to Marty's greeting each day, "Good morning, boss."

His mother also sensed that all was not well with her son. She tried to talk to him and find out what was really going on behind the mask he was wearing. Mike assured his mother he was fine and her worries were soon assuaged when he met Caroline.

One sunny summer day Mike decided he needed to get out of the dealership. Usually he stayed in his office, but today he needed to get out for some fresh air and to enjoy the sunshine and light summer breeze.

"Hey, Marty. Are you ready for a break? I could use a fountain soda from Dalton's. I'll drive."

"Sounds good to me."

They got in Mike's car and drove to Dalton's Drug Store. They sat on the green vinyl stools at the soda counter and ordered two Cokes.

"So how's everything going with you?" Marty checked in with Mike every so often. Mike's quiet and withdrawn nature concerned Marty. On the side, Mike's father shared his son's story with him, and although he was proud of his son, he also was blind to his pain. Marty noticed the faraway look in Mike's eyes and the strained look on his face as soon as he walked into the dealership for the first time, and then every day since.

"Okay. I'm getting the hang of the business."

"You're good at selling cars, and your dad sure is proud of you."

"I know. He tells me every day how proud he is that I'm working with him. He wants to turn the company over to me some day."

"Your dad built a successful business, and I'm sure he's happy that all his hard work will go to you some day. Who knows what would happen without you. It could all go to waste."

"It's just not what I expected to be doing with my life."

"I didn't plan on doing what I'm doing either. I thought I'd be living in Morocco working the Grand Prix, but then I met Jean and all of that changed, for the better I might add."

"I know. You have a great life, though. You have an amazing wife and you still get to work on racecars, and I'm pretty sure that if I weren't around my dad would turn the dealership over to you."

"When you meet the woman of your dreams, everything will change for you, too. You'll see you're exactly where you need to be."

They finished their drinks. "Listen, I need to pick up something for my mom. Do you mind if we look around?"

The pair found their way around the drug store and finally stopped at the perfume counter. Mike felt a little guilty for hiding the truth about feeling depressed lately and maybe a nice bottle of perfume would relieve that guilt. What he didn't expect was that the conversation he just had with Marty was about to come true. Mike was engrossed looking in the glass cases at the perfume boxes and fancy bottles when Caroline approached him. Marty stood off to the side, willing his friend to work a little of his charm.

"May I help you, sir?"

Mike looked up and his eyes met Caroline's. He smiled and leaned on the counter knocking over a perfume display.

"Oh, gosh. I'm sorry."

"It's okay. This happens all the time. This is a bad spot for a display." Caroline took some cleaning supplies from under the counter, hoping this attractive and sweet customer wouldn't be scared off by some spilled perfume.

He reached for the paper towels, "Here, let me clean this up." *Real smooth,* Mike berated himself as he wiped up the glass.

"Why don't we start over? May I help you?"

Mike tried to think of something clever to say, but Caroline was so pretty that he stumbled over his words and all he could get out was "I'm buying something for my mom."

Mike glanced over and saw Marty shaking his head. *Gosh, that sounded so stupid,* Mike thought. *She probably thinks I'm some kind of momma's boy now. Why couldn't I just say something cool?*

"Aw. That's so sweet."

Mike looked back at Marty, who this time winked and nodded his head in approval.

"What kind of perfume does your mom wear?"

Mike relaxed a bit. "You know, I'm not sure."

"Okay. Well, then why don't you try some out and buy her something you like."

"That's a good idea."

Caroline took a few of the tester bottles and sprayed them in the air for Mike to try.

"No favorites yet?" Caroline smiled. "How about this one?" Caroline saved one of her favorites for last. She took the small bottle with the white cap from the shelf and sprayed its fine mist on her wrist, lifting her left hand toward Mike.

Mike's face met Caroline's delicate wrist. "Mmm...I do like this one."

"I thought you might." Caroline winked. "Would you like it wrapped?"

Mike waited while Caroline wrapped the box in white floral paper. Mike paid for the gift and thanked Caroline, then headed to the door where Marty waited.

"Go back and ask her out."

"I can't ask her out. Did you see how pretty she is?"

"Yes, she is pretty and she is interested in you. She let you put your face all over her wrist for crying out loud."

"I didn't have my face all over her wrist. Okay, maybe a little."

"No woman who isn't interested in a man sprays perfume on herself and then lets him smell her. Go back and ask her out."

"I can't. Let's just go."

Before pushing the door open, Mike turned around and looked back toward the perfume counter. Caroline was still standing in the same spot looking at him and smiling.

Marty blocked his exit. "I can't let you leave, boss, until you ask her out."

Mike turned around and walked back to the counter, fully intending to ask Caroline out for the next evening but he heard himself say instead, "Do you have plans for tonight?"

"*Tonight?*" Caroline was caught a little off guard with the unexpected offer, but she was thrilled. "Actually, I am free this evening."

"May I take you out to dinner?"

"Yes. That would be lovely. I work until five today."

"I'll see you then."

Mike turned toward the door and signaled success to Marty.

Marty put his hand on Mike's shoulder. "Attaboy, boss. When's the date?"

"Tonight."

"Whoa. *Tonight?* My boss is a stud."

Mike laughed and for the first time in a long time, he felt happy.

Mike returned at five to pick up Caroline for dinner. They drove to Howard Johnson's and sat for hours talking about their lives. He hadn't planned on opening up to Caroline, but talking to her was so easy. She was kind and attentive and with her blue eyes and dark hair; Mike couldn't stop looking at her. Mike told Caroline the story of his hearing, how when he was younger, his mom would call him for dinner and he couldn't hear her. He would get in trouble for being disrespectful and he shared with Caroline how hurtful that had been to him as a child. Finally, Mike's mom began to suspect something was wrong. One time they were in the same room and he had his back to his mom. She asked him a question and he didn't respond. Mike turned around to see his mom in the same room and he jumped, not knowing she had been there. After that Mike found himself at the doctor and after the diagnosis, she took him for ice cream and apologized for all the times he got in trouble for not listening. Mike's mom had tears in her eyes; he put his arms around her waist and hugged her. *It's okay, Mom.*

As Mike talked, Caroline realized she could barely notice his hearing loss. Talking to him face to face there seemed to be no problem at all. As the evening came to a close, Caroline hoped Mike would ask her out again. She hoped he had as much fun on their date as she had. They drove back to the drug store so Caroline could get her car. He opened her door for her. "I had a wonderful evening with you. How about I pick you up at your house tomorrow and we try out the new diner up the street?"

"I would love that."

Caroline's parents liked Mike from the moment they met him. When they returned from their second date, Caroline's parents invited him in for some lemonade. A grand piano sat in the living room calling Mike's attention to it. "This is a beautiful piano. Who plays?"

Caroline's father answered. "Sadly, none of us. It was my intention that we would learn to play as a family, but my job took me out of town so often that the few lessons we took only yielded a sorry rendition of 'Twinkle, Twinkle, Little Star.'"

"Would you mind if I played?" he asked, motioning toward the piano.

"Please do."

Mike sat at the piano and played "When You Wish Upon a Star," and as he sang the lyrics Caroline and her parents joined in. The evening went on with Mike playing Glenn Miller and Tommy Dorsey songs. Two hours later after several "play just one more" pleas in hopes of continuing the evening, Mike and Caroline said their goodbyes for the night.

They spent every day of the next three weeks together. Mike's parents loved Caroline and Mike finally felt happy; the burden of his lost military career lifted. The thought of having a new life with a tender, beautiful, caring woman compelled Mike to buy an engagement ring. He told his mom about his plans and asked her to help him pick out a ring. A week before the proposal, Mike asked Caroline's father permission for the marriage. Caroline's parents were thrilled that they would be adding a son to their family. Mike made the engagement a family affair, planning a dinner at Caroline's house along with his parents. There would be a fancy dinner on the porch and singing around the grand piano after. He planned on saving the song "If I Had You" for last. Immediately after the last note, he would get on his knees and present Caroline with the diamond ring.

Mike carried the ring around in his pocket everywhere he went, every once in a while checking to make sure it was still there. The ring represented a new prospect in his life and that new prospect was happiness. The more time he spent with Caroline, the deeper he fell in love with her. The way Caroline tilted her head when she listened to Mike's stories made him feel like he was the only person not just in the room, but in the world. He dreamed of what the next few months held for the two of them. Mike had saved up enough money to put a down payment on a house, and he could just imagine the look on Caroline's face when they found their future home. Because of his father's business, they could have the pick of any car they wanted in the lot. Although Mike's plans for the military took a different turn, with Caroline in his life he was beginning to believe he had a real future ahead of him.

The day of the engagement, Mike arrived at Caroline's first followed by his parents. Caroline's father stood out back grilling steaks while her mother set the picnic table. Low humidity made the mid-summer day feel more like early autumn with the sun sending rays to warm the body and the wind a breeze to cool it back down. Caroline had set up a game of croquet to enjoy after dinner in some friendly family competition, and the flat backyard with freshly mowed grass provided ample space to set up a challenging course. Although Mike's family was competitive, they held back a bit to allow Caroline's family to win. The generosity of steaks on the menu and the hospitality of hosting the impending engagement made Mike's family want good vibes flowing well into the evening.

As the sun began to set, Caroline's father suggested they all go inside to listen to Mike play a few songs. He opened up with "Happy Days are Here Again" followed by "Pennies From Heaven." He seemed collected on the outside, his fingers moving seamlessly over the keys without a hint of nerves in his voice, but on the inside his stomach was rolling over and over. To prevent himself from breaking into a sweat, Mike decided to speed things up and play the song for Caroline next.

"I learned a new song that I would like to try out. It's a newer song, but I think you'll get the hang of it." Mike began playing "If I Had You" while everyone began joining in slowly. Caroline picked up the song quickly and her face lit up as she sang the words. When the last note was sung, Mike stood up from the piano stool, took a box out of his pocket, and got down on his left knee. Caroline put her hands up to her mouth.

"Caroline, you are the woman of my dreams. You have made me happier than I ever thought I could be. It would be my honor to have you for my wife. Caroline, will you marry me?"

"Yes!" She threw her arms around Mike and they hugged and laughed while their parents smiled and clapped for the happy couple.

Caroline looked down at the ring on her finger and then around the room. "Were you all in on this?"

"Maybe," Caroline's mother answered with a smile.

The next few weeks were spent planning the wedding. It would be an outdoor wedding at Caroline's parents' house. She chose yellow and white for her colors and ordered daisies for the centerpieces and for her bouquet. A string quartet would play through dinner and dancing later in the evening. Marty would be Mike's best man.

When Caroline wasn't working or planning for the wedding, she and Mike looked for houses. Touring development after development still didn't yield their start-up house, let alone their dream house.

One Friday morning Mike walked into the dealership looking a bit discouraged.

"Why so glum, boss?"

"Caroline and I just can't find a house to move into once we're married. It's getting a bit frustrating, Marty."

"Why didn't you say so? There are two houses for sale right near Jean and me. How about you and Caroline come over tomorrow afternoon for a cookout and to take a look at the houses? We live in a great neighborhood. I think you'll like it."

"You know what? I think we'll do that. Thanks, bud."

The next day Mike and Caroline drove to Marty's house. As they toured the neighborhood, they noticed all the houses were very different from each other, but every one of the homes offered its own brand of character.

As they parked their car in the street, Jean and Marty walked across the front yard to meet them.

Jean and Caroline, who had never met, took an instant liking to one another.

"I made some fresh lemonade and iced tea. We can sit on the porch and talk for a bit before lunch."

"That sounds nice," Caroline replied as they made their way to the side porch.

"It is so quiet and private here," Mike remarked. "I get a good feeling here. What do you think, Caroline?"

"I do, too." Caroline knew she was getting her hopes up, but this place was different than all the rest. She hoped the houses they would be seeing had the same comfort level as Jean and Marty's house.

The four new friends talked over refreshments, with Jean doing most of the conversing.

"Right across from us lives a Reading baseball player."

Mike's interest was piqued even more. "Really? Who?"

Marty answered. "Eddie Getz."

"You're kidding! I saw him play. Why didn't you tell me this before?"

"I guess because he's just a regular guy to us."

"Oh, man. This is quite the place you live. When will the real estate agent be here?"

Just as Mike finished the question, the agent pulled up.

"Here he is now." Jean motioned toward the street.

"I am so looking forward to seeing these houses. I hope we're not disappointed again." Caroline looked hopeful in Mike's direction.

Jean assured her. "You'll love this place. The hard part will be choosing which house suits you best."

After the introductions, Jean said, "We'll wait here for you." They sank back into the patio chairs enjoying the feel of the sun warming their faces.

The real estate agent took Mike and Caroline to tour the house three doors down. The house had a whitewashed brick exterior with gray shutters and a black front door. Once inside, the house featured highly polished light hardwood floors, a formal living room, three bedrooms, and two baths finished in mosaic tile. A brick patio sat off the back of the house sporting a built-in outdoor fireplace. Quiet up to this point, Mike broke the silence. "What do you think, Caroline?"

"I really like this place."

"We have one house on our list."

The real estate agent looked hopeful. "Let's take a look at the next house."

The trio walked to the second home, which sat across the street from the house they had just toured. It was on the same side of the street as Eddie and Elizabeth's house a few doors up. The stone home offered cherry hardwood floors and a view from every room in the front of the house. This house was bigger than the last, with a gourmet kitchen, four bedrooms, and three bathrooms.

Mike asked Caroline, "Can you see us living here?"

"I really didn't think any other house could top the last one we just saw, but this one is a dream. I can definitely see us living here. Just look at this view."

Mike inquired about the price.

"This house is twenty thousand more than the first one."

The disappointment on Caroline's face sank Mike's heart. "The first one was really nice, too, Mike. That one will make a nice home for us."

The agent knew when he needed to give a couple time alone. "I'll wait out front for you. Take your time, look around again if you want; we'll talk in a few minutes."

Mike had always been good with money, a lesson he learned from his dad. Mike actually had enough money to buy both homes if he wanted.

Mike put his arms around Caroline's waist and drew him to her. "Which house does my bride want to start our life together?"

"I want us to start out life together happy. Twenty thousand dollars is a lot more money and I don't want that to put a strain on us."

"Let's look at the view one more time." Mike and Caroline stood at the living room window. "You can see Jean and Marty on their porch down there. It looks like they're having a second glass of lemonade."

Caroline laughed.

"Let's go upstairs and take a look at our bedroom."

Mike led Caroline upstairs. "This is where I'll carry you on our wedding night. We're so high up, we don't even need curtains. Well, maybe we do need curtains. I want that night and every other night of our marriage to be special." Mike ran his hands through Caroline's hair and kissed her. "What do you say?"

"I really like this house, but it's so much more money."

"I never want to see you upset or disappointed. If money were no object, which house would you want?"

"This one. It would be a dream come true."

Mike took Caroline by the hand and led her out of the house to the front lawn where the agent waited.

Mike said, "We'll take it."

Caroline threw her arms around Mike's neck.

"Congratulations to both of you. Excellent choice."

Taking his bride-to-be around the waist, Mike smiled. "Let's go tell Jean and Marty."

As they crossed the street, Jean and Marty stood up and Marty yelled over to them. "Well, are we neighbors?"

"We're neighbors."

Jean jumped up and down. "Which house?"

Caroline beamed. "The stone house on the hill."

"That's absolutely gorgeous. You will be so happy there."

Jean poured fresh glasses of lemonade and iced tea for everyone. She held up her glass.

"To friends and to many happy memories together. Cheers."

Over the next few weeks, Mike and Caroline moved their belongings into their new house. Besides being a quaint neighborhood, the new development was situated a few blocks from Main Street. They would be within walking distance of a corner store, a few restaurants, and a bar. As the weeks rushed by, they still each lived with their parents until the wedding, but Mike and Caroline would sit for hours on the sofa in their house looking out over the hills and talking about how their life together was going to be.

"We are going to have the perfect life together, Caroline."

Placing her head on Mike's shoulder, Caroline asked, "How do you know?"

"I know because we love each other and because nothing in my life seemed right until the moment I met you."

Their storybook life carried on for the next few months. The wedding was well attended. They spent a week in Cape Cod for their honeymoon, and shortly thereafter Mike and Caroline were expecting their first child. The neighborhood proved to be the right fit for them. They easily made friends with some of the neighbors and enjoyed cookouts and back-yard fun even through the late fall months.

The day everything began to change for Mike and Caroline was the day life changed for most people in the modern world. The attack on Pearl Harbor headlined the papers and seeing the country thrust into the throes of war brought back all the wounds about his health and the military that Mike thought were healed. There wasn't any place he could go that the war wasn't the topic of the conversation. Men and women signed up to serve their country and everyone did whatever they could to be of service. Once the government halted the production and sale of automobiles, Mike and his dad's business changed, with the dealership seeing the last car to be sold off the lot two months after Pearl Harbor, but the car manufacturer had seen this coming and had begun to train the dealership workers in mechanics. Mike and his father collected scrap metal to ship to Detroit for military construction. While their business thrived, other dealerships closed their doors. Mike's dad bought two of those dealerships and hoped for the best after the war.

In June Mike and Caroline welcomed their new baby boy, Christopher. Mike spent most days at the dealership processing and shipping the scrap metal, while Caroline took care of Christopher. It was near the end of the summer when Marty and some of the other guys from the neighborhood decided to try out Shorty's, the bar on Main Street.

Mike called Caroline, who seemed so tired on the other line that he was about to say, "No, you guys go ahead without me," but then Caroline chimed in, "You've been working so hard. Go ahead honey. Christopher and I will be fine until you get back."

They met up at Mike's house. "You ready, boss?" Marty asked. "We're going to walk since Shorty's is only a couple of blocks away."

He was a little reluctant to leave his new family for a night out. Not only had he never been in a bar before, Mike had never taken a drink before, but Marty knew the bartender and when they walked in and Shorty said, "Hey fellas. Good to see you. Have a seat. Have a seat," Mike began to relax. A few of the other neighborhood guys were there. Mike had never met them before; they lived around the block and Mike didn't venture away from the familiarity of the guys on his street. Shorty poured a whiskey for the men. Mike watched as the others lifted their glasses and swallowed the drink in one gulp. He did the same and for as much as the whiskey stung his throat, it also took away the pain he'd been feeling these last few months. Working as a car salesman was far from what Mike had really wanted to do in life, but he forgot all about that when Caroline came along. He felt he could work at any job as long as he had Caroline in his life, but now his failure was thrown in his face daily. Most of the staff, mechanics and salesman, had all enlisted in the Army. Now it was just Mike and his dad and a few others working the scrap. Each day handling the metal that would be sent for military use reminded him of what he really wanted to be doing with his life. Months of feeling hopeless and desperate slowly faded away with each drink. He was finally happy and grateful for the relief.

At closing time, the three friends walked back to their homes. When Mike arrived at his house, Caroline was in bed, asleep. He checked on Christopher and then slid into bed next to Caroline. He slept soundly the next few hours and when he woke up the next morning, his first thought wasn't his wife or his baby son, it was of his next glass of whiskey.

Caroline gave Mike a good morning hug. "Did you and the guys have fun last night?"

"We did. It was nice to get out."

"Well, I'm glad you had fun. You've been working so hard and this is such a tough time right now."

"It is, but we'll get through it."

When Mike arrived home later that day after putting in ten hours of work, he and Caroline enjoyed a nice dinner together. He played peek-a-boo with Christopher and ran his son's bath water. After Caroline was ready for bed, Mike said, "Since you're ready for bed, I'm just going to head down to Shorty's for a little bit."

"Are you meeting the guys again?"

"Um, no. I mean, I don't know if they will be there or not."

"Mike, it was one thing for you to go yesterday, but to go again tonight? That's just not like you."

"I've been under a lot of stress at work. I just think this will really help me relax."

"I don't like it Mike, and I don't want it to become a habit."

"Don't worry. It won't." Mike kissed Caroline on the cheek and walked out the door. Once inside the bar, Shorty greeted him as he did the others the previous night. "You're back. Have a seat. It's Mike, right?" He could feel the tension drop from his shoulders. This is what he needed. This would make everything better. Four hours later Mike stumbled back to his house. He checked on Caroline and Christopher. Both asleep. All was well. He slipped into bed and fell fast asleep.

For the next few months, that was how Mike made it through life. He went to work, spent some time with his family, and when they were in bed, he made sure they were safe and locked in the house and then he went to the bar. The country was approaching the anniversary of Pearl Harbor and the weather was growing cold. Mike came home from work as usual, but when he pulled up to the front of the house, Caroline was waiting on the porch.

"Is everything okay, Caroline?" He asked as he got out of the car.

"Not if you call my being pregnant fine."

"You're pregnant?" Mike picked up Caroline and spun her around in a circle. "That is the happiest news. We have to call everybody."

"Stop it, Mike. I'm not happy about this at all."

Mike's smile fell from his face. "How can you not be happy?"

"Maybe because you're out every night at the bar drinking and I'm home alone with our son."

"I don't need to do that anymore. I'm sorry. I'll stay home every night. I want you to be happy."

"Do you promise?"

"Yes, I promise."

"I'm still really mad at you, Mike. You shouldn't have spent all those nights at the bar."

"I know and I'm sorry." He kissed Caroline on the cheek. "Forgive me?"

Caroline smiled. How could she stay mad at Mike? He was her husband and their family was growing. "I forgive you."

"Good. Now let's tell everyone our news."

Mike kept his promise for the next few years. He was there for Caroline as they cared for Christopher and their new daughter, Cece. As the war drew on, Mike and his father continued to use their business for the war effort, and even though he couldn't be on the front lines, it gave him some satisfaction to be aiding in some way. The war years passed and finally the auto sales ban lifted and Mike and his father began selling cars again. It didn't take long for him to sink into despair once life returned to normal. With the war over Mike felt the harsh reality of lost dreams creep up once again. The sale of each car reminded him of how hard he worked to overcome his hearing loss, but to no avail. The military didn't want him. Caroline was too busy with the kids to notice his despair. They were school-aged now and there was homework and other activities. Mike began to think about how to relieve some of this pain. Since his kids were older and Caroline was tired at the end of each day, he thought perhaps heading to Shorty's for a quick drink once everyone went to bed would be the answer; after all it had helped in the past.

It was a Thursday night. Mike was sitting in the living room reading when Caroline walked over to kiss him good night.

"Since you're going to bed, I'm going to head down to Shorty's for a drink."

"Okay. Are you meeting the rest of the guys there?"

"Maybe. I'm not sure who's there."

"Well, be careful."

That was easy, Mike thought. He walked out the front door, down the street and around the block. It didn't take long to walk to Shorty's, and in no time he was sitting at the bar with a glass of whiskey in his hand. Taking the first sip was like catching up with an old friend. They knew each other well and although they hadn't seen each other in years, it was like they had not spent any time apart. This old habit came back to Mike easily, and night after night he spent hours at Shorty's drinking whiskey, sitting quietly at the bar while his wife and kids were at home.

CHAPTER 21

I wish life was not so short...

—J.R.R. Tolkien

Jean closed her eyes. "I need to rest for a minute."

"Rest for as long as you need. Do you want me to get a nurse?"

"No. That's the last thing I want. I just need a minute to rest."

Maggie looked calm on the outside but on the inside her mind and emotions raced. Her throat tightened and tears rolled down her face.

Jean opened her eyes. "Honey, don't cry. I'm old and tired. I told you I had the best life a girl could have, but it's time for me now. I have no regrets."

Maggie put her face in her hands and unable to hold in her emotions, she sobbed.

"Jean you can't go. You're my only friend."

"Maggie, we'll always be friends. All you have to do is look out your window toward my house and think about all the talks and memories we shared. You know, I was so lonely before you moved in. You filled these last few months of my life and I've been happier than I've been in a long time."

Maggie gathered herself together for her friend. In the past each time Jean told her stories, Maggie couldn't wait to hear more. So she did what she had always done and asked for more of the story.

Maggie's voice was still a little strained from crying. "What happened next?"

"Remember the party I told you about at Elizabeth's house? The one when we all went to the Apple Dumpling Festival?"

"Yes."

"Well, on our way there, I asked Caroline if everything was okay. The back of my house looks out over the hill Mike used to walk down every night on his way to Shorty's. I think both Caroline and Mike must have thought it was late enough that no one would notice, but I did. I saw him going to the bar and on some nights when I couldn't sleep and I stayed up late, I would see him walking home. When I told Caroline this, she started to cry. She said she didn't know how she was going to keep living with Mike drinking every night. She was lonely and didn't know how to help her husband or their marriage. She felt like everything was slipping through her hands and she couldn't hold on anymore."

Jean closed her eyes again, this time longer than the last.

She began again. "That pattern went on night after night until…" Jean started to cry. "Oh, Maggie. What happened next is…" Her voice broke off and her crying became a whimper.

"It was in the newspaper."

Maggie was having a hard enough time losing her only friend, but to see her so upset was more than she could bear.

She wanted Jean filled with happy memories. "You know what, Jean? I'll look the story up and read it myself. Let's talk about your happy memories now."

"No, Maggie. This is something I've been waiting for. Nothing we talk about will change the outcome, but I do want to help you in these last moments. That will bring me peace. You need to know what happened to Mike and Caroline."

Maggie took a deep breath. As difficult as this would be, she needed to pull herself together for Jean.

CHAPTER 22

We do not err because truth is difficult to see.
It is visible at a glance.
We err because this is more comfortable.

—Alexander Solzhenitsyn

Snow fell all day, and as Mike and Caroline watched the snow accumulate outside their picture window, Mike reeled at what the next day held: scraping windshields and clearing snow off every car in the lot. Sure, he had help from the other salesman, but the sole responsibility of the business rested with Mike.

Caroline sat on the sofa with her legs folded under her quietly sipping a cup of tea. "It's so peaceful here, Mike. The only sound is the wind outside. We made a good choice coming here so many years ago. With the kids older and able to do more on their own, it's nice to just be able to sit with you and enjoy our time together."

Mike didn't answer. He was still thinking about all the inventory that would need to be cleared.

"Mike?"

Shaking himself out of his next day's work, "Yes, it was a very good decision to move here."

"Is everything okay, Mike?"

"Sure. You know how it is, though. This snow means a whole lot of work for me early tomorrow morning."

"Why don't I come in and help?"

"I'm not having my wife clear snow off cars. No way."

"I'd be happy to help, Mike. I'm always happy to help you."

"I appreciate your offer, Caroline. I really do, but there is no way I'm having my wife doing the work that is my responsibility."

"Things aren't the way they used to be. Women work now, and it would make me feel good to help you."

"Thank you, Caroline, but the answer is still no."

Caroline so desperately wanted to know what was going on with Mike. She thought maybe if she spent some more time with him she could get him to open up to her. He seemed so distant and so preoccupied. She worried about him. Making the only other offer Caroline knew Mike would accept, she asked, "Would you like me to make you some coffee?"

"Now, that I would love."

Christopher and Cece came downstairs from their bedrooms and sat in the living room with their parents. Cece curled up in a chair next to the sofa where her parents sat and Christopher sat on the ottoman at his father's feet. Turning to his father Christopher asked, "Tomorrow morning all the kids from the neighborhood are going sledding. May we go too?"

"It looks like tomorrow will be a snow day. Sure, you may go sledding with your friends."

"Thanks, Dad!" Christopher and Cece said in unison before running back upstairs to their rooms.

"Why don't I make a nice dinner for us tonight? Pot roast, mashed potatoes, and candied carrots? I think I have enough flour to make a cake, too."

"That sounds like just what I need on a snowy day. A home-cooked dinner will help me get through tomorrow morning, that and a cup of coffee."

"I'll get up with you and make a good breakfast, too. I can't have you clearing off an entire lot full of cars on just a cup of coffee."

"That would be nice. Thank you, Caroline."

Mike stood up and leaned over to kiss his wife on the forehead. "I have a few phone calls to make to my staff. I'll be in my office."

Mike closed the door to his office. Life just wasn't what he wanted it to be. He loved his family and adored his wife, but these day-after-day doldrums took a toll on him. How was he contributing to anyone in any significant way in life? The military would have provided that opportunity for Mike. He would have protected and served the country. Each day of not fulfilling his destiny wore on Mike. It got harder and harder to get out of bed in the morning and go to a job that he was beginning to dislike more every day.

Mike listened to Caroline in the kitchen, opening and closing cabinets and drawers. He heard the timer on the oven buzz indicating it was ready for the roast. Caroline tried everything she knew to help Mike. She made him feel like a million dollars by telling him how important his job was. Mike was fair and honest and kind. People felt relaxed coming to his dealership. People worked hard for their money and Mike didn't take advantage of them. It was his father's philosophy and Mike carried it on. Still, it wasn't enough for Mike.

In the kitchen Caroline hoped that her dinner along with the snow would keep her husband home this evening. She was tired of spending her nights alone, and to top it off, Jean and Marty saw Mike from their house walking to Shorty's late at night. Caroline felt embarrassed that her husband was leaving his family each night to sit at a bar with a bunch of men he barely knew. At first Caroline had thought Mike was having an affair, and maybe in a way he was, just not with a woman. With a bottle of whiskey. Caroline didn't understand how she and the kids weren't enough for him. What was making him so unhappy that his only solace was in a drink? Caroline tried talking to Mike, but he was unreceptive. He explained that being at Shorty's helped relieve his stress and he didn't feel like he was taking time away from his family since he only went to the bar after everyone was in bed.

As dinnertime grew closer, Caroline set the table. Mike joined her and poured water for everyone. He called the kids to the dining room and the sound of Christopher and Cece's footsteps running down the stairs made Mike smile. "Okay, okay. Manners please. Mom spent all day making dinner for us, so let's show our appreciation."

Christopher and Cece took their seats as Caroline carried the roast to the table. Christopher said, "It looks delicious. Thanks, Mom."

Cece followed, "Yes. Thanks, Mom."

Mike always started the dinner conversation with "How's school?"

Cece said, "I have a book report due at the end of the week. I'm halfway finished with it."

Christopher responded, "I have a project due in history next week. After dinner I'm going to get a head start on my research."

"It sounds like everything is going well for the two of you."

Christopher said, "It is. Both of us have straight A's and report cards are coming out soon."

"Make sure you show me. A's get a higher rate than other grades."

Cece smiled. "We know. Why do you think we have straight A's?"

Caroline chimed in. "How about because you want to succeed in life and doing well in school is a start?"

Still smiling, Cece said, "That, too."

"You're silly, Cece." Caroline patted Cece's hand and smiled back at her daughter, thinking of how blessed she was to have such sweet kids. The neighbors thought highly of both kids and Caroline was so grateful they were close siblings. Christopher and Cece didn't argue and they always looked out for each other.

Each night went this way. A nice dinner. The family together. Caroline hopeful that Mike would stay home. But it always ended the same way. The kids in bed, Mike would make his trek down the walkway from the house, across the street, down the hill behind Jean and Marty's house, making a right at the bottom, and eventually crossing the main road to get to Shorty's. Although Mike's pattern continued, Caroline couldn't help but think, *Maybe tonight will be the night. Maybe tonight we're enough for him.* Once again though, Caroline would stand at the picture window watching the flashing sign at Shorty's, knowing her husband had chosen a drink over his family. Each night close to tears, Caroline tried to find the answer in her heart. *Maybe if I were thinner. Maybe if I were a better cook. Maybe if I wore fancier clothes.* No matter how much effort Caroline put forth at being perfect, Mike's nightly routine didn't change.

After dinner Caroline made coffee and poured milk for her children. Caroline and Mike sipped on coffee while they enjoyed the chocolate cake Caroline baked earlier.

"Thanks, Mom. This is the best cake you ever made." Cece rubbed her stomach. "Yummy in my tummy."

"It's great, Mom." Christopher agreed as he took his last forkful of cake.

"May we be excused? We have some work to do tonight so we can go sledding tomorrow."

"Yes, you may. Just take your plates into the kitchen first."

With Christopher and Cece upstairs, Mike said, "I'll wash the dishes. You worked hard on all this today."

"I'm just glad everyone enjoyed dinner and dessert. It's okay. You have a busy day tomorrow. I'll take care of the dishes."

"We'll do them together."

Mike dried the dishes as Caroline washed them.

"Would you like to play cards or maybe sit and read?"

"Whatever you want to do, Caroline."

"I thought it would be nice to sit and enjoy each other for a while. It's cold outside and we're all snug in the house."

"Okay. Let's play cards."

Caroline and Mike sat in the living room. They played cards, drank coffee, and talked about the snowfall. Finally, Christopher and Cece came downstairs to say goodnight to their parents.

"Good night, sweethearts," Caroline said while giving her son and daughter a hug.

Usually Mike stood up and said, "Goodnight," but this time after standing up he said, "I'm proud of you two. You're the best kids a father could have. I love you both." Mike hugged Cece and then Christopher.

"Thanks, Dad. I love you, too." Christopher responded first.

"I love you, too, Dad." Cece said.

As they ran upstairs, Mike turned to look out the picture window and the flashing sign at Shorty's caught his attention. *I didn't think he'd be open tonight,* Mike thought.

Mike walked to the entryway closet to grab his coat.

Still standing in the living room, Caroline more commanded than asked, "Where do you think you're going?"

"I'm going to head to Shorty's for a bit. I didn't think with the weather and all he'd be open, but the sign is flashing so someone has to be there."

"You know what, Mike? I've had it. I have tried everything to be a good wife to you. I make dinner for you every night. I support you in every way I can to make your job easier. I try to look good when you come home no matter how tired I am and no matter what kind of day I've had.

I never bring any of my stuff up to you. I figure all my problems out on my own, and I don't bother you with any of it because I know how tough your day was. I try to make everything in our lives perfect, but there's one big part of it that's not perfect and it has nothing to do with me and it has nothing to do with our children, but it has everything to do with your drinking. Don't think for one minute because you never drink in our house and you always leave that somehow it's okay and somehow that means you don't have a problem, but you do. You have a problem, Mike."

Mike could feel anger welling up inside of him. "You have no idea what you're talking about."

"Yes, I do. You sit down at Shorty's for four hours every night. You don't leave until closing time. How much do you drink when you're there? Some mornings you can barely get up. Maybe that's why you hate your job so much. Maybe it has nothing to actually do with your business, maybe it has to do with your drinking. Maybe that's what's making you miserable."

"What's making me miserable right now is you."

Caroline looked like she had been slapped across the face. Mike didn't talk to his wife that way. He loved Caroline. Panic overcame Mike. "Caroline, I'm sorry." He tried to take her gently by the arm, but she pulled away.

She turned around with tears spilling from her eyes, feeling this was the beginning of the end of their marriage. "If you go to the bar tonight, you are going to lose me and the children. I'm not doing this anymore."

"You're overreacting. I'll be back soon. I just want to say hello to the guys."

Caroline stood with her back to Mike as he walked out the front door, the snow still slowly falling to the ground. Caroline made her way upstairs, got her suitcase out of the closet, and threw it on the bed.

Mike walked down the front path from his house to the street below. He wore his dress shoes, probably not a good idea with the depth of the snow. They would definitely be ruined, but he could just get a new pair in a day or two, plus he had others he could wear to work.

As he passed by Jean and Marty's house, he was unaware his two friends watched as he made his way to Shorty's once again.

Jean turned to her husband. "I'm concerned about him, Marty. This isn't good. Every night he does this, but tonight of all nights. I'm worried about their whole family. Caroline must be in agony over this."

Marty threw open the kitchen window. The snow that fell upon the window now worked itself onto the window ledge inside the kitchen. Marty yelled to Mike. "Hey, Mikey. Where you going on a night like this?"

"Just heading out for a walk. I have a long day tomorrow and I need to clear my head."

"You're not heading to Shorty's are you?"

"Just going for a walk, Marty."

"Do you want some company?"

"Nah. I'm good."

"Call me if you need me. I'll be there bright and early tomorrow. Heck, I might have the cars cleared off before you even have your first cup of coffee."

"Now that sounds good to me, Marty."

Marty closed the window. Jean asked, "What do you think? Should we go after him?"

Considering the despondent tone of Mike's responses, Marty said, "I think that would be a good idea. Let's get ready."

Mike crossed the main street in front of Shorty's with no wait. A usually busy road, empty tonight. Everyone was home safe. Too dangerous a night to drive. The jukebox played softly to the three men sitting around the bar. Crowded for a night like tonight.

The bartender greeted him first. "Hey Mike. I didn't expect to see you here tonight. I thought you'd be home with your beautiful wife."

The truth was no one could believe Mike would leave someone like Caroline home alone night after night. What a turn of events. Mike could barely believe Caroline had agreed even to go out with him so many years ago, and now here he was married to a beautiful woman, leaving her on her own.

"Ah, you know. I have a tough day tomorrow. Thought I'd unwind a bit."

Mike didn't have to order. The bartender brought him his usual. Whiskey, straight up.

Mike looked at his drink, but didn't lift it to his mouth.

"Something wrong?"

"No. Not really."

"Come on, Mike. I've known you for years."

"It's just a day like today makes me think of how much my life got off track."

"You're married to one of the most beautiful women I've ever seen and you have two of the best kids a man could ask for. Compared to other men I know I'm not sure how off track your life really is."

"It's owning the car dealership and not fulfilling my plans of being part of the military. I'm just getting so frustrated. The older I get, the more a reality it is just how far away I am and ever will be from attaining those dreams."

"Mike, being in the military isn't the answer to everything. Do you know that most guys who sit around this bar each night are war veterans? The war has been over for years, sure, but do you know how much baggage those soldiers carry with them? The nightmares. The changed personality. The inability to relate to family and friends. It's all taken its toll. Most of them end up in a bar somewhere to try to forget the ordeal. They witnessed terrible things. Things no one should ever have to see, and here you are upset because you didn't get to go."

Mike stared at his drink. "I guess I never really looked at it that way."

"Do you know how many men would love to own a car dealership? How many soldiers are finding it difficult to even find a job let alone carry on the day-to-day responsibilities of holding one?"

Mike began to feel convicted. All of this self-pity and time wasted.

"Why don't you take the opportunity you've been given to make the money you make and do some good with it? These men need help. I'm telling you, they have nowhere to turn. No one wants to hear about their bad dreams. Their flashbacks. Their ruined relationships. I don't know—what if you started some sort of foundation to help veteran soldiers? How would that be for fulfilling your dream?"

Mike let the bartender's words soak into his being. "I guess I've been too wrapped up in my pain to see anyone else's. You really have something here. I mean, something special. You're right. I could help."

"Think about putting the pieces together. They'll all fit somehow. But for now, start by getting home to your family. To your beautiful wife. Most women would have kicked you out by now."

The bartender took Mike's untouched drink and poured it into the sink. "You've been a good customer, Mike, but what's right is right. Go do something good with your life."

For all the times Mike staggered out of Shorty's in a stupor, this was the one time he staggered out without the help of alcohol, but with the intoxication of life and of the possibilities ahead of him. As the blast of cold air filled his lungs and the sting of the snow hit his face, Mike closed the front door forever. Never would he go back. Mike buttoned his coat and drew his scarf close about his neck as he made his way down the sidewalk. The flashing light of Shorty's lit his way for a short distance as he made his way to the street. Mike stopped at the curb and looked up in the direction of his house. On a clear night he could see his house bathed in the outdoor lights Caroline left on for his return, but tonight he could only make out a faint hue. Mike stood on the curb reveling in his future and that of his family. The ones who had always been there for him even when he unintentionally tossed them aside. Standing in the snow piling up around his feet, Mike sent up a message to them. *I'm coming home.*

Jean and Marty changed out of their pajamas. Thinking this evening would be a night at home relaxing by the fire, the boys had retired to their rooms early and Jean and Marty got comfortable for a night at home, but seeing Mike walk to the bar on an evening like this one screamed *intervention.* Jean asked Marty, "What's the plan?"

"I'll start the conversation and then any time you feel you need to jump in, please do."

They left the house through the back door and headed down the hill in the direction of Shorty's. In the distance they could see the shadow of the flashing light that had enticed Mike night after night, year after year.

Five miles away Grant steered his tractor-trailer the best he could. The snow and ice mix on the road made it difficult to maneuver, and the only part of the evening that provided a bright spot is that no one else was on the road. He only had two more runs to make before retiring. Next week, he would be on an island somewhere enjoying the fruit of all the hours logged on the road. The job had had its ups and downs and tonight was definitely one of those downs. Grant strained to see in front of him, but ice coated the windshield after every swipe of the blades. He kept his speed slow and steady in this weather, feeling unsure of this vehicle that he had grown to know so well over the years. Looking forward to being at home, he approached the familiar section of Main Street in Wyomissing Hills. Usually at this point his trailer load was empty, but with the bad weather the warehouse guys had gone home and Grant was left to haul a full load to his house to wait until tomorrow's delivery. He was sure his neighbors would not be pleased to have a truck this size parked in the street and he hoped he didn't impede the next day's snow removal. The radio station softly played filling the cab of the semi with the song "If I Only Had You." Grant's wife loved this song and every time it came on the radio, she stopped everything and held out her hand until he danced with her. Only a few more miles and he would be home with his wife. She always had something warm waiting for him. Table set and his wife of thirty years waiting for him never got old. Grant pushed the thought out of his mind; he needed to concentrate on the road and the rest of his ride. Grant leaned closer to the windshield trying to see as far ahead as he could. Finally, in the distance Shorty's flashing light marked his way. Only a few more minutes and he would be home.

Staring up at his house, Mike stepped from the curb into the icy street. Consumed with thoughts of his wife and how she had stayed by his side, he didn't think to look for cars, and with his hearing loss, he never heard the sound of the truck approaching.

As the wipers cleared the windshield, Grant caught a glimpse of a lone figure crossing the street. He pumped the brakes slightly, but instead of coming to a stop the truck started sliding right into the path of Mike. Grant hit the horn again and again. To him the sound of the horn blared into the night, but to Mike it was a faint sound in the distance— still, he looked up. As the truck slid closer, Mike tried to get out of the way, but the ice and snow made getting out of the way impossible. Still trying everything he could to keep the truck from hitting the man, Grant pumped the brakes and gripped the steering wheel. Mike was still scrambling to get out of the way when the grill of the truck hit him. The sound of Mike's body against the metal cut through the night. When the truck finally came to a stop, Mike lay still on an icy bed in the middle of the road.

CHAPTER 23

As a well-spent day brings happy sleep,
so a life well used brings happy death.

– Leonardo da Vinci

Jean stopped talking for a moment and let the tears run down her face. Maggie took a tissue and dried Jean's tears.

"Maggie, it was the worst moment in all my life. Marty and I were half a block away and we saw the whole accident. We watched as the truck came down the road and as Mike stepped into the street. There was nothing we could do. We started to yell, but the sound of the wind drowned out our warnings. I'm not sure Mike would have heard us even on a clear night."

Maggie had tears in her eyes. "That is so horrible."

"It was awful. I don't even know how Marty and I made our way to Mike. I don't remember a single step, I only remember kneeling next to him. He was still alive and trying to talk. I took him by the hand and said, 'You're going to be okay, Mike.' Marty put his hand on his shoulder and told him to hang on. Marty said, 'Help's on its way.' Mike's lips kept moving like he was trying to tell us something. I said,

'Take your time. It's okay. Everything is okay.' It took him a while to say this, 'Tell Caroline and the kids I love them. And tell Caroline I wasn't drinking. I was coming home to her. I'm sorry.'"

Jean began crying again and this time Maggie didn't try to hold back her tears. They held on to each other's hands and cried together. A nurse quietly walked into the room. She looked at the monitor next to the bed and put her hand on Jean's arm. "You're getting ready for your journey."

Maggie wanted to stand up and yell, *No. Don't go Jean. Stay here with me.* But she kept silent as the nurse spoke quietly. "You're getting ready to see Marty. It's been a long time, but soon you'll see him."

"I'm looking forward to that." Jean answered. "I keep telling my friend Maggie that I had the best life a girl could have."

The nurse smiled. "I bet you did. Well, I'll leave you two friends alone for a bit. I'll be just outside if you need anything." The nurse put a comforting hand on Maggie's shoulder and that moment gave her strength to gather herself.

Jean seemed to gather more strength herself and continued the story. "Marty and I stayed beside Mike. We knew he was dying so we talked to him about playing the piano for us soon. I said, 'Soon we'll all be together with your beautiful wife right next you as you play the piano for us. We'll sing and we'll dance and we'll…'"

Jean got quiet for a moment. "Those were the last words Mike heard and when he passed there was a smile on his face. I could hardly imagine a smile at that time, but it was the thought of Caroline. I know it."

"What happened to Caroline and the kids?"

"It was a difficult time as you can imagine. Caroline fell apart when Marty and I told her what happened. I think the fact that Mike wasn't drinking and he was coming home to her kept her from getting angry. She was sad, sad all the time, and eventually it was too emotionally draining to live in a house that looked out over the accident scene. Caroline and the kids moved to California and after that we never heard from her again." Jean rested for a moment. "Maggie, I'm telling you all this because you need to forgive your husband and get your marriage and your family back together. Get rid of all this pain and bitterness and resentment. It's not worth it."

"I know, Jean. It's just so hard to let my guard down."

"I'll tell you what's hard, Maggie. Living life without your husband. That's hard. All these years without Marty…"

Maggie didn't want her friend suffering these last few moments. She wanted Jean's journey to be peaceful. "Jean, you're right. I promise you that I will make amends with Scott. I will get my family back better and stronger than we've ever been. You have no worries about that. I promise." Maggie took Jean's right hand and held it between both of hers.

Jean raised her hand to Maggie's face. "That's what I wanted to hear. An old woman knows about life."

"Thank you, Jean. For everything. For your friendship and your stories. For caring about Abby and me and spending time with us." Maggie's voice cracked.

"Thank you, dear. Spending time with you and Abby. You made my last few months happy."

Maggie began talking quietly to her friend. "Now let's talk about the first time you saw Marty. Remember how beautiful you looked and you had just won more blue ribbons than anyone else that day when you spied a group of men all looking at gorgeous you but there was one who stood out among all of them, your husband. Marty picked you up from your house and took you to dinner. He knew the moment he saw you that you would be his wife."

Jean closed her eyes and a smile spread across her face as Maggie continued, pausing, allowing time to let the memories in.

"Remember your first date...the band playing in the background...dancing under the stars..."

Jean listened closely and allowed Maggie's voice to take her away to the happy times in her life, the time when she still had her husband, and as Jean slipped away, joy and peace filled her as did the vision of Marty taking her in his arms and twirling her around and around under the stars, with each spin transforming them into their younger selves. Jean looked like a movie star and as Marty, tanned and youthful, spun her in his arms, her floral gown moved about her body, flowing with the momentum of the two lovers, and as the music softly came to an end, still in their embrace, they gazed into each other's eyes and smiled.

Maggie sat for a moment with her friend. Jean's smile told her that she had passed with happy memories. For a moment Maggie felt comforted by that, but then a flood of grief filled her, and she put her hand on Jean's arm and her head on the side of the bed and sobbed. She wasn't sure how long she had been there when she felt a hand on her shoulder. The nurse stood behind her with tears in her eyes. "Is there anything we can get for you?"

"No. No, I'm fine."

"Stay as long as you need."

After the nurse left, Maggie folded her hands and placed her elbows on the side of the bed. *Dear God. Thank You for Jean. Thank You for her friendship. I pray that Jean is with You and that she's singing and dancing and happy. Amen.*

Maggie left the hospital and drove home in a daze. Scott met her at the door, but the way she walked up to the house with her head down, he knew.

"Honey, I'm so sorry." Scott wrapped his arms around his wife.

"I can't believe she's gone." Maggie cried on his shoulder, happy to be in his strong embrace.

The family held a small memorial service. Maggie and Scott attended, listening to the stories of a mother and grandmother. To hear Jean's family talk about how much she meant to them brought back her words. Her family had been everything to her and with the sadness of the past few days, Maggie realized she had let an opportunity go by to talk to her husband and try to make everything right between them.

When Maggie and Scott got back to their house, Ellen sat on the front porch swing holding Abby. Maggie was grateful to have such a reliable young person in her life. When the news spread of Jean's death, Ellen called and said she would watch Abby any time she needed. Maggie could hear her daughter laughing as soon as she got out of the car. Ellen greeted them. "How did everything go today?"

Maggie answered, "It was a sad day, but we heard a lot of comforting stories about Jean and her family. We're happy to be home. How did everything go here?"

"We had a picnic lunch out back on the patio. Abby's stuffed animals joined us. Then we went for a walk around the block, and then we sat on the front porch swing. Abby's very tired but she's been fighting sleep. I think she was afraid she might miss something good out here."

"Thank you for taking such good care of her."

"It was all my pleasure." Even though Ellen didn't want to accept payment for watching Abby, Maggie insisted.

"You gave up a big part of your day to help us out. We really appreciate all the work you did."

Before Ellen left, she gave Abby a kiss on her cheek. "Bye-bye, sweet girl."

Ellen waved as she left. Scott took the baby upstairs for a nap and then joined Maggie on the porch swing.

She said, "I keep thinking about Jean and all of the stories we heard today. How do you live your whole life and then meet your end that way? It's so sad."

"Death is sad. It's sad for all of us left behind. And the ending isn't pleasant. Whether it's an illness or an accident, seeing a loved one pass away is heart-wrenching. I think all we can do is when we're blessed enough to be able to spend the end with someone, we make sure their passing is peaceful. That's what you did for Jean. You were there for her and I'm sure your being there brought her great peace and comfort."

Maggie's eyes filled with tears as she thought about Jean's end and how thankful she was to have talked to Jean about happy memories as she made her journey. Scott had been so supportive through all this. She remembered a time when they could sit and talk for hours and being here on the porch reminded her of those times.

"You know, I've been a complete wretch these past few months."

"Maggie, this has been a stressful move for all of us. Moving to Pennsylvania was not in our plans, and I'm just sorry that the job didn't work out in Montana."

This was her Scott. The kind of man who smoothed over all her bad behavior, forgiving her when she felt like she could never be forgiven, and worse yet like she shouldn't be.

"We should have the kind of marriage that it doesn't matter where we are as long as we're together, and I shouldn't have acted like I did. I am so sorry. It just pains me to look back over the past few months and think of the way I behaved."

"Don't look back over that time, then. When you think of our first months here, just think about Jean and the time you spent with her. You really were a blessing to her."

Maggie began crying again. It had only been a few days, but she missed her friend so much already.

Scott put his arm around Maggie and drew her into his chest.

"I'm sorry, Scott. I'm sorry for the way I acted."

"Look at me. I want you to forget about all of this. I could have done a better job, too. I was so hurt when I didn't get the job in Montana that I became all wrapped up here in having the accolades from the college administration to the point that I didn't even think about how stupid it would be to have an assistant and not tell you. And—not to mention how I didn't see Bridget for who she was until the party. Like Jean said, men just don't get it sometimes."

Maggie started to laugh a little and then her laughter turned into all-out hysterics, half laughing and half crying. Maggie finally caught her breath. "Did Jean say that to you?"

"It wasn't so much her words as it was her tone."

"When was this?"

"A couple of days after the president's party, Jean waited for me one morning."

"No!"

"Yes. She had a few things she obviously wanted to say to me."

"Like?"

"Like, *ditch the assistant.*"

"Jean was always looking out for us."

"Yes, she was."

"I think maybe we reminded her of when she and Marty were younger and they had all their friends in the neighborhood. Before Jean passed away, she told me about Mike, one of their friends. There was a bad accident and Jean said it was in the paper. Do you think maybe sometime we could go to the library so I could read the article?"

A few days later Scott and Maggie packed Abby's diaper bag for a day out and headed to the college. As they pulled into the library parking lot, Maggie commented on the architecture of the buildings.

"I only saw part of the campus the night of your colleague's party, but this looks like an Ivy League college during the day with the old stone buildings, mature trees, and cobblestone walkways."

"This is actually considered a sub-Ivy League college. It looks impressive on a résumé and it really is a top-notch college. I'm lucky to be here especially without having written any books yet. I think they must have seen the potential in my research and it's been going very well. I should be able to put my findings together to publish in the next few months."

"That's fantastic. I am so proud of you." He had worked so hard for this position, and Maggie was grateful to the administration for acknowledging his work.

"Thank you."

As Maggie let go of the resentment she had been feeling toward Scott, she felt the burden lift from her shoulders. She felt happy and secure in her marriage and confident about their future together. So much healing had taken place between them these past few days.

As they walked up to the steps of the library, a few of Scott's students stood around the courtyard talking. When they saw their teacher, they waved and yelled over to him. "Good morning, Professor."

Scott introduced his students to his wife and daughter. The girls were taken with Abby and said, "We'll babysit any time you need us to. She is *so* adorable."

"Thank you for the offer. Maggie and I need to get out and explore the area a bit more."

"That's true. We haven't been able to get out much, but I think that's changing now." Maggie smiled at Scott.

Once the family entered the library, Scott showed Maggie the microfiche room. One of the librarian's assistants helped her, but without knowing what year Jean had been talking about or Mike's last name, Maggie had to guess so the search took some time. Finally, she came across a headline, TRAGIC ACCIDENT TAKES LOCAL MAN'S LIFE. Maggie began reading the article. "Monday evening at 11:45 p.m. while crossing the street in front of Shorty's Bar, Michael Moyer was hit by a truck and killed. Authorities blame icy road conditions for the accident. The driver will not be charged. Mike leaves behind his wife, Caroline, and two teenage children."

Maggie sat in front of the screen rereading the article. So few details. It dawned on her that Mike Moyer had lived a life and the article didn't provide any of that. It made her sad.

"Did you find what you were looking for?"

"Kind of."

"What does that mean?"

"Jean told me so much of the story of Mike's accident and death, but the article is only a couple of sentences. Here this man had a whole life, but it was summed up in a few short words. It doesn't tell the story of the man or his family."

"What happened to Mike's wife after the accident?"

"Caroline had two teenage children and Jean said they all moved to California."

"Looking at Abby it's hard to think about her being a teenager. I wonder where we will be when our daughter's that age."

"I don't know where we'll be, but I do know that we will be together."

Scott put his arm around Maggie and hugged her.

CHAPTER 24

Love is when he gives you a piece of your soul,
that you never knew was missing.

−Torquato Tasso

The family arrived back home to a hub of activity in Jean's front yard.

"What's all this?" Maggie asked Scott as they pulled into their driveway.

Scott read a sign placed by the sidewalk on Jean's property. "Public Auction. Saturday, 9:00 AM."

"Ugh. This can't be happening. Look at all of Jean's stuff." Maggie watched as one of the auction workers carried the gazing globe across the yard. "Scott, that gazing globe. Jean wanted me to have it."

Scott got out of the car and hurried across the street. "Excuse me, sir."

"Yes?"

"My wife and Jean were friends and Jean wanted my wife to have that gazing globe."

By this time Maggie had gotten Abby out of her car seat and stood next to her husband.

"Sir, Jean told me months ago to take the gazing globe."

"Ma'am, I'm sorry, but our orders are that everything gets auctioned. I can't give you the globe. The best you can do is bid on it Saturday morning along with everyone else."

"This is my friend's gazing globe and we used to sit on her porch and watch the bluebirds in its reflection. It reminds me of my friend and she wanted me to have it."

"Sorry. Like I said, the auction is Saturday morning."

Maggie wanted to say more to the man, wanted to give him a piece of her mind, but she was too close to tears; one more word and the flood would start.

"Let's go, Scott." Maggie walked back to the house with Abby while Scott stayed behind for another minute.

"Listen. My wife is telling you the truth."

"Sir, I wish I could hand this over to you, but the executors of the estate want everything sold."

"Okay, so do you know what time on Saturday this will go to auction?"

"It's an antique so it will be one of the last items sold because of its value."

"Thank you."

Saturday morning came around. Scott got up early and took care of getting his daughter ready for their big day at the auction. He put Abby into her baby carrier, and they walked down to Jean's house where the auctioneer was just stepping up to the microphone. The front yard was filled with Jean's belongings, and as Scott walked down the sidewalk he saw the items extended to the back yard, as well. The street was lined with cars and a few cargo vans with antique dealer logos. Scott's heart sank. He was glad he brought the checkbook.

Maggie slept longer than usual that Saturday, and woke up to the sound of the auctioneer's voice. Rising from her bed, she walked to the bedroom window, which looked out over Jean's house. Seeing all the people walking through Jean's yard going through all of her personal belongings made Maggie ache for her friend. *So this is what happens in life? We spend most of our lives acquiring things and then we die and people go through our stuff trying to get the best bargain possible? Jean would be sick about this.*

Maggie couldn't bear to watch the auction and she started away from the window until she saw Scott walking across the street with Abby in her baby carrier, and her husband carrying a big box. He put the box down on the front walk and looked up at the window and gave his wife a thumbs-up sign.

Maggie opened the window. "What are you doing?"

"I bought some stuff. Come down. I think you'll enjoy this."

"I'm not going to enjoy the auction. It makes me sad to see this. I'm going to go in for a shower."

"Abby and I will be here if you change your mind."

"I'm not going to change my mind. I'm going to put on loud music and take a shower."

Scott took Abby's little hand and made a waving motion to Maggie. "See you soon, Mommy."

Maggie smiled and closed the window. Once in the shower Maggie cried thinking about the times she spent with Jean, and how she taught her so much about life. What matters is people, not things, but there were so many memories wrapped up in Jean's things. Everything Jean had, she kept over the years because it reminded her of Marty, or her family, or her friends. After Maggie got out of the shower and looked in the mirror, her swollen, red eyes sealed her decision not to go to the auction. Instead, she took her time getting ready and sat in the back room, far away from the front of the house and the sounds of the auction.

Scott walked around Jean's yard while waiting for the auctioneer to put the gazing globe on the block. He noticed several men standing around the gazing globe, which sat in a secure corner of Jean's porch. Scott had already won bids against these men, whom earlier he had seen sitting in the antique dealers' cargo vans. He was determined to win the gazing globe. After half an hour, the auctioneer put the gazing globe on the block, describing it before he set the price.

"We will begin the bidding at $250. Do I hear $250?"

The starting price shocked Scott, but he put the auction paddle in Abby's hand and helped her raise it in the air. Ten other paddles went up at the same time and the group of ten battled it out until the price hit the $400 mark. Half dropped out, and Scott thought, *Won that battle. Now it's time to win the war.*

When the price of the gazing globe hit $500 the bidding dropped to Scott and one other man, an antiques dealer.

Abby laughed each time Scott helped her raise the paddle and people standing near them had a double show, the bidding war and the adorable baby. Scott saw the strain on the dealer's face and feeling relaxed, he whispered to Abby, "Time to bring the gazing globe home."

The auctioneer raised the price by twenty-five dollars twice with both paddles going up. Then, another twenty-five.

"$575, do I hear $575?"

Scott nodded as he and Abby raised the paddle. Abby giggled, and when Scott saw no contest from the other bidder, he said quietly to Abby, "You can laugh even harder now, sweetie. That gazing globe is ours."

"$575, going once, going twice. Sold!"

Scott raised both of Abby's hands in victory. Everyone except the antique dealer laughed. It might not have been the best auction etiquette, but Scott was determined to have the gazing globe, and once the bidding war started he prepared to go much higher. People congratulated him while the last two items were auctioned off.

Scott wrote a check to the auctioneer for all his purchases. The worker from the other day wrapped the globe in bubble wrap and placed it gently in a box. "I'm glad you won. I felt so bad about not being able to give this to you."

"One gazing globe, $575. A happy wife—priceless."

"This is going to make her very happy."

Scott carried the box back to his house and put it on the dining room table. He called out to Maggie, who appeared from the great room in the back of the house. "Can you take Abby for me? I need to get another box from outside."

"What did you do?"

"You'll see."

Scott placed the other box on the dining room table. "Let's put Abby in her highchair and let her snack on some Cheerios while you see what's in the boxes."

Abby played with the Cheerios on the highchair tray, content, as Maggie opened the first box.

Inside of the first large box were two smaller boxes, but both still rather big. Maggie opened the one on top first. She took out the delicate blue ribbons and held them in front of her. "Oh, Scott. Jean's ribbons from the horse shows. Jean loved these. Oh my. Thank you so much. I feel like I'm going to cry." Not wanting the dam to break again like it did this morning in the shower, she held back the tears the best she could.

"You and Jean love horses. It's fitting that you have them. There's more. Open the next one."

The box on the bottom had more weight to it, and the contents were carefully wrapped in tissue paper. Maggie gently took off the paper and a delicate white teacup with little blue flowers stared up at her. "Jean's teacup collection." And at that Maggie sat on a dining room chair, put her head on the table and cried.

Scott put his hand on her shoulder. "It's okay, Maggie."

"I'm going to get it together. This is just so unexpected. That little cup was the first one I used when we had coffee together. Jean always let me pick."

"There's more in the box."

Maggie spent the next few minutes carefully opening each teacup. The next was the red and black cup with the gold trim that Maggie also loved. Scott had bought Jean's entire collection, including the saucers.

"I thought we could clear out the corner hutch," Scott said motioning behind him, "and we can display the teacups there."

"It will make me happy seeing them all the time."

"You have one more box to open."

Looking at the box, Maggie stood up and turned to Scott. "It's the gazing globe, isn't it?"

"I can't tell you what it is. You have to open it."

"If it's the gazing globe, I'm going to cry and I just stopped. Knowing ahead of time will prepare me."

"It's the gazing globe."

Maggie ran to her husband, threw her arms around his neck, and cried against his chest. "Thank you, Scott." She caught her breath and gathered herself together.

"Are you ready to open it?"

"Yes." Maggie opened the top of the box and lifted the globe from it. She unwrapped the bubble wrap and held the gazing globe in her hands. "This means so much to me. That you did this for me."

"I love you, Maggie, and I want you to be happy."

"I am happy. I love you and Abby and we're going to have a wonderful life here."

CHAPTER 25

Ne'er look for the birds of this year in the nests of the last.

—Miguel de Cervantes

A year went by. The "For Sale" sign in front of Jean's house now read "Sold." Scott finished his research and published his findings. Maggie volunteered once a week at a local homeless shelter. Abby learned to walk and to say a few words.

Early one morning, before Abby woke up from her sleep, Maggie and Scott tiptoed to the dining room to enjoy the quiet of the day over a cup of coffee. Maggie chose a teacup for each of them, for even Scott began drinking his coffee from Jean's teacups.

She looked out the window. "You can see the whole yard from the gazing globe."

Just then a small bluebird landed on top of the globe.

"Maggie, look."

"I see her."

The bluebird sat looking in the window, whether she was staring at her reflection or at Maggie and Scott, they didn't know, but what a blessing to have her there.

"I hope she stays. I followed all the directions when I hung the bluebird box."

"And I planted raspberry bushes to give her a food source. We did everything the book said to do."

They watched as the bluebird made her way into the box. "Scott, we did it. Do you know how hard it's supposed to be to get bluebirds to nest in your yard? But there she is."

Later that morning a moving truck pulled up in front of Jean's house. A young couple got out of a car that followed behind, and the husband went to the back seat to get their baby boy out of his car seat.

Scott commented to Maggie, "Looks like our new neighbors are here."

"Yes. It does."

"Maybe you could invite the wife over for coffee."

"And maybe I could serve the coffee in Jean's teacups."

"And maybe you can tell her stories about the woman who used to live in their house."

Just then the bluebird came back and sat on top of the gazing globe.

"Blue Jean's back." Maggie said.

"Blue Jean?"

"That's what I'm going to call our bluebird, Blue Jean, and every time I see her I'm going to think about Jean and her life and how she saved us."

"We have a lot to thank Jean for."

Maggie sat on the window seat in the dining room, sipping coffee from a teacup and watching the reflection in the gazing globe of the young couple starting their new life together. In time they would all be friends, the couple across the street and Maggie and Scott. And as the older generation moved on and new people moved into the neighborhood, they would include them, and they would support each other, encourage each other, laugh together, cry together. And one day many years from now when they were all old and gray, a young couple would move in a few doors down and they would share with them the stories of what used to be. But for now, Maggie had her family back—together and stronger than ever. Just like she promised.